W9-CUF-503

TRAPPED!

The lights in the office were out. Julie unsnapped the small flashlight she carried on her belt and focused it on the file drawer. She flipped through the letters to the R's.

Reilly, Riskin, Robinson . . . She kept on through Rolfe, Rumford, Rundel, and there was the S file. Pat Robbins's file was missing.

The overhead light went on with such a dazzling shock she let out a cry. Rick was standing there. It seemed like a century before he spoke. "What are you doing, Julie?" His voice was like iron.

"I was looking for Pat's file." Her voice shook. The expression in Rick's eyes scared her. He moved toward her slowly, his silence more frightening than anything he could have said. She was sure he was going to kill her.

MOONSTONE novels for you to enjoy

Available from ARCHWAY paperbacks

Most Archway Paperbacks are available at special quantity discounts for bulk purchases for sales promotions, premiums or fund raising. Special books or book excerpts can also be created to fit specific needs.

For details write the office of the Vice President of Special Markets, Pocket Books, 1230 Avenue of the Americas, New York, New York 10020.

MOONSTONE™
MYSTERY ROMANCE

WHEN DARKNESS FALLS

BARBARA CORCORAN

AN ARCHWAY PAPERBACK
Published by POCKET BOOKS • NEW YORK

This novel is a work of fiction. Names, characters, places and incidents are either the product of the author's imagination or are used fictitiously. Any resemblance to actual events or locales or persons, living or dead, is entirely coincidental.

AN ARCHWAY PAPERBACK *Original*

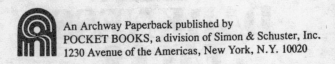

An Archway Paperback published by
POCKET BOOKS, a division of Simon & Schuster, Inc.
1230 Avenue of the Americas, New York, N.Y. 10020

Copyright © 1985 by The Cloverdale Press and Barbara Corcoran
Cover artwork copyright © 1985 Gary Lang

All rights reserved, including the right to reproduce
this book or portions thereof in any form whatsoever.
For information address Pocket Books, 1230 Avenue
of the Americas, New York, N.Y. 10020

ISBN: 0-671-54452-7

First Archway Paperback printing November, 1985

10 9 8 7 6 5 4 3 2 1

AN ARCHWAY PAPERBACK and colophon are
registered trademarks of Simon & Schuster, Inc.

MOONSTONE is a trademark of The Cloverdale Press.

Printed in the U.S.A.

IL 5+

WHEN DARKNESS FALLS

Chapter 1

A cool morning wind blew off the Rocky Mountains as the last notes of the bugle call for Assembly died away. Children and counselors poured out of the buildings of Camp Bitter Root, converging in the big log cabin where assemblies were held. Sixty children from ages five to twelve were running, skipping, dawdling, some coming from the Hash House still clutching a half-eaten piece of toast, some running back to their cabin for a sweater, one stopping to tie the laces of her Nikes. The older girls hung back to walk with the boys, while the smaller ones skipped along the curving path to keep up. Rick, the camp director, was popular, but everyone knew he was strict about keeping rules.

And one rule was that campers should be on time for meals, Assembly, flag-raising, Taps. He liked to know where people were.

Julie looked around the cabin where she was head counselor. It was in its usual morning mess. But clean-up time came right after Assembly. "Hurry up, Pat," she said to one of the girls who lived in her cabin. "You'll be late again." It was Julie's first year as a counselor at Bitter Root after having spent several years there as a camper. It was still hard for her to act like a disciplinarian.

Pat was unhurriedly brushing her beautiful blond hair in front of the mirror. At eleven, Pat was not only beautiful but, Julie thought, so much more sophisticated than she herself was, that it was hard for her to lecture Pat about anything. Sometimes Julie got the uneasy feeling that Pat was really older than *she* was.

"Come on, Pat, get with it, will you?"

"Julie." Pat used the tone of sweet reason that she saved for grown-ups who were being unreasonable. "You want me to look good, *don't* you, in these new clothes my dad sent me from Paris—keep up the cabin image and all that?"

Julie managed not to say that she really didn't care whether Pat did her new clothes justice or not. As for the cabin image, she glanced down at her own faded khaki shorts and her navy and cream tattersall shirt with a button missing. What a contrast to Pat, who was wearing a deep purple silk turtleneck, monogrammed

2

of course, and pleated white shorts that almost screamed "Expensive!"

"We're going on a cookout this afternoon, don't forget. You're just going to get them all sweaty and dirty. It will be hot. And sandy."

"I never perspire," Pat said, carefully applying eye shadow.

"Then you're not human" Julie replied exasperatedly. Really, Pat was too much sometimes. While Julie was genuinely fond of her, Pat also frustrated her more than any other camper. Who else had a father who bought her clothes in Paris as he floated through on his way to a picture-taking safari in Africa? "He's promised me a set of carved ivory elephants," Pat had said. Just what every eleven-year-old girl wants for her birthday—carved ivory elephants! But Pat's mother was dead and Father coped by sending her to boarding schools—anywhere from Switzerland to California—and by lavishing money, clothes, and gifts on her. Pat adored him, although it was Julie's impression that she didn't see much of him.

Julie left the cabin and caught up with her friend Sandy on the U-shaped path that curved around the end of the long, narrow lake. "Pat will be late again," she said breathlessly. "I guess I shouldn't lose my temper with her, though. That's not How to be an Effective Counselor." Rick had given them a series of lectures at the start of the season, on what he expected of the counselors, what they should strive for.

"Oh, it won't hurt her," Sandy said. At just five feet tall, dressed in ragged cut-offs and camp T-shirt, she looked like a camper herself. Her red hair was pulled back in a ponytail. "She's spoiled, Pat is."

"I know, but she's basically a good kid. I think she's lonely. Sometimes she cries herself to sleep, and when I ask what's wrong, she says, 'Nothing. Just my hay fever.' "

"Maybe it is."

"She doesn't have hay fever."

Sandy was silent for a moment, then ventured, "I suppose she needs more love, like all of us."

Julie grinned. Sandy was probably the most loved counselor in camp, and her mailbox bulged with letters from admiring boyfriends. "Too bad you're so emotionally deprived."

Sandy turned up her freckled nose. "Ain't it the truth."

Julie glanced out at the lake. Both water and sky were intensely blue today. The reflection of the sun on the water was dazzling, and suddenly Julie felt full of energy. It was a good day for the cookout.

A nine-year-old named Hamilton Chester came charging past them. "Last one to Assembly is a rotten, putrid, stinking egg."

"Ham's got a terrific crush on Pat," Julie said. "Though he wouldn't be caught dead admitting it."

"Poor little guy. I suppose Pat thinks of him as a baby."

"More like a gadfly. She ignores him, and he shows his devotion by teasing her."

"Unrequited love is tough."

They followed the crowd into the long, low-roofed log cabin that served as assembly hall, theater, gathering place for groups, movie house on Saturday nights, chapel on Sundays, and sometimes the scene of an ice-cream party. The lake side was almost solid glass, with huge windows that latched open like the windows in the cabins, so that on a fine day like this one it was almost like being outdoors.

At one end there was a small stage and at the other end a big fireplace made of Montana's beautiful rocks, combining colors of pink, red, lavender, and cocoa brown. Above the fireplace was an enormous mounted buck's head with wide-spreading antlers like branches. Along the side wall there was a grizzly head that looked a little moth-eaten, a mountain goat's head, and a nineteen-pound, red-striped rainbow trout. Julie's dad had said the place looked like a Montana bar. But then neither he nor Julie was big on hunting. Instead, they liked to go out together and shoot animals with their cameras. When she was younger she and her cousins had learned to shoot a .22 on her uncle's ranch, but she didn't really like guns, and she hated the idea of killing beautiful wild animals.

Behind the assembly hall, off to the west, pine and spruce and western larch crowded close on the camp property; still further in the background, mountains rose, some of them wooded, some bare. As August approached, the wind from those mountains was beginning to take on an early morning chill. The day before, Julie had seen a V of Canadian geese fly over. Summer would soon be gone, but she had her first year at the university to look forward to.

Julie and Sandy slipped into a couple of seats in the third row, behind two male counselors, Mark Haney and Joe Cooke. Sandy made a face at Mark's back, and Julie giggled. Mark was a cool, rather distant young man from New Hampshire, about to begin his second year at Yale. Rick, a Yale graduate, was working on his doctorate there, and he had taught a freshman English class that Mark was in. Julie guessed that they'd gotten to know each other in that course, which had led Rick to hire Mark as hiking and mountaineering counselor. Water sports and mountain-climbing were the camp's specialties.

"It's odd," Julie had said to Sandy, "that Rick hired Mark, because sometimes I get the impression that they don't really like each other."

"Rick is practical," Sandy had argued. "He'd hire the guy who could get the job done. Mark has a lot of Appalachian experience, and the kids love him."

Julie looked at Mark, admiring his attractive profile in spite of herself. Those long-lashed blue eyes, the brown hair that curled just a little . . . Too bad he was so remote. Maybe he had a girlfriend back East.

But Joe, at least, was far from remote. Almost as if

he'd read her mind, he swiveled around in his chair, with his wide, friendly grin, and put his hand on Julie's arm. "Hey, is this the day of the big cookout?"

"Sure is. You want to come?"

"I can't." He made a tragic face. "I have to take a bunch of tenderfeet on a ride to Beaver Dam." Julie smiled back at him. Joe was good-looking, too, and he was also one of the two big football stars on the Grizzly team at the University of Montana. Julie was impressed with him and flattered by his attention. He'd be a senior in the fall, four years older than she was. She hoped he'd date her when they were on campus.

The kids in her cabin teased her about Joe's attentiveness. "Joe, Joe, the buffalo, he grab Julie and away he go." That was Pat's brilliant contribution. She and the others liked to chant it at the most embarrassing moments.

Unexpectedly, Mark turned around and spoke to Julie. "I'm taking some kids up Thorne Mountain this afternoon. They're pressuring me to join your cookout. What do you think?"

"There you go," Joe said, "horning in."

He was kidding as usual, but Mark turned pink and said, "Only if you feel you can handle it, of course."

Julie's feeling of pleasure at his suggestion died. Why did he have to be so touchy? "Sure you can come. How many?"

"Ten."

7

She did a little quick arithmetic. "Okay, there are twelve of us, two in each canoe, so there'll be room coming home. I'll bring twice as much food."

"Thanks." Mark glanced at Joe's hand still grasping Julie's wrist. He frowned and turned away.

Dana, the head water sports counselor and Julie's boss, came in and sat next to Julie. She was about twenty-five years old and taught anthropology at a Utah college during the rest of the year. Some of the children thought she was too strict, a little too sharp, but on the whole, Julie liked working with her. Dana had taught her a lot about water sports and about handling kids, and she was helping Julie with her self-confidence.

"All set for the trip?" Dana asked. It had been her idea to let Julie take on an outing of her own.

"I think so." Julie told her about the addition of Mark's group.

Dana frowned. "Kind of last-minute," she said in a low voice.

"It's okay." Julie crossed her fingers. "I can deal with it." She hoped she was right. Only minutes ago, she'd been worrying about her own group, hoping she wouldn't make any mistakes. Her group was made up of campers who had recently passed lifesaving tests that allowed them to paddle a canoe by themselves, as long as a counselor was around. The logistics of planning and preparing a cookout for a dozen people was unlike anything she had ever done, and Julie was very anxious to get it right. Now there would be twice as many people. But maybe it would give her a chance to know Mark better. He couldn't be as indifferent as he seemed, or the kids wouldn't like him so much. Maybe you had to be twelve or under to get his attention.

There was a stir as Rick came in a side door. The camp director was a good-looking man in his late twenties who seemed to have the right touch when it came to one-on-one relationships. Every child, and counselor too, was made to feel as if Rick knew and cared about him or her, and that he was concerned with making each one happy. It was a gift, especially in the kind of job he had here.

Julie saw that Rick had a friend with him. The visitor was a short, dark man, older than Rick, dressed in clothes that looked citified and a bit flashy in this setting: carefully pressed gabardine trousers, a dark red button-down shirt, and an Argyle wool vest. He and Pat should get together, Julie thought—a couple of clotheshorses. She looked around to see if Pat had arrived. No sign of her. Darn! Rick was unusually tolerant of Pat. Sandy said it was because her old man was "stinking rich," but even so, he was bound to get annoyed about this late business.

Standing up near the front of the stage, Rick smiled at his captive audience. Julie shifted in her seat; she never felt quite as comfortable with him as she would like, even though he was very nice to her. It was her own self-consciousness, she was sure, that made her uneasy. She wanted so much to do a really good job as a counselor. For one thing, it would help with college expenses if she could be a counselor for the next three summers.

Even though he was young, Rick had had plenty of camp counseling experience and had been head counselor for several years at some camp in the East. The owners of Camp Bitter Root were an elderly couple who had a string of camps all over the Northwest. They had visited a week ago, had obviously been pleased with the way everything was being handled, and had taken off for Europe.

"Good morning." Rick gave the group a sweeping glance that made each person feel his smile was just for them.

"Good morning," the campers chorused.

"I see some of you got through flag-raising and breakfast and you're *still* looking sleepy." He waited for the laugh. "Well, I'll try not to disturb your slumber too much. But we have the usual announcements to make. And I want to introduce my old friend Alfred Peterson. Al and I go a long way back. Al, say hello to the gang."

Al Peterson waved, and the girls clapped.

"Now," Rick said, "what have we here." He consulted a small slip of paper. "The usual arts and crafts class at ten. Archery for team members only, team members only today, at eleven. Dana will take over Julie's afternoon swim classes so we can spring Julie for the cookout." He was interrupted by cheers. "Betsy"—he turned to the small, serious crafts counselor—"did you have something to say?"

Betsy jumped up. "Yes. Please be prompt and wear old clothes. We're going to finish up and fire this morning. All Project Two people, be on time. And that means you, Eloise."

The tall ten-year-old named Eloise giggled, and endured pokes and remarks from her friends. Betsy sat down.

"Joe," Rick said, "got something for us?"

Joe lumbered to his feet. From Julie's viewpoint, just behind him, he looked as broad and solid as a rock wall. "The Beaver Dam bunch will leave from the stables at three o'clock on the nose. You all know who you are. We won't get back till lateish and it could cool off, so bring sweaters or something. You should be there and have your horse saddled by three-oh-five. I thank you, ladies and gentlemen." Making a mock bow, Joe sat down, his chair creaking noisily under his weight. He got a small round of applause.

Julie's hands were damp with nervousness. She had never had to make an announcement in Assembly before. She hoped she wouldn't get tongue-tied.

There was a slight commotion at the back of the hall,

and she knew before she looked that her camper had finally arrived. Pat came in quietly, but there was a buzz of comment on her new clothes.

Rick looked at her for a moment. Then he said, "Pat, you and I are going to have to have a heart-to-heart talk about your remarkable inability to tell time."

"I'm sorry," Pat said meekly.

Julie was surprised that Rick let Pat off so easily. She had expected some kind of punishment, since this was the third time this week that Pat had been late.

"Julie," Rick said, "do you have some words for us?"

She stood up and immediately forgot to be nervous. She reminded them that departure time was four-thirty—"On time, or you'll get left behind"—and then explained about the addition of Mark's group. She appointed Mary and Jennifer and Mason and Ham to help her load the canoes. "And don't forget sweaters. It will be dark when we come home, and chilly." She got a cheer as she sat down. *That wasn't bad at all,* Julie thought with surprise. *All you have to do, is concentrate on your job, and then you forget to be nervous.* Important lesson learned. She'd have to tell her mom, who was always telling her she was too quiet.

She glanced at Dana, hoping for a nod of approval, but Dana was gazing at the back of Mark's neck with a small dreamy smile. Julie felt a pang of . . . what was it? . . . irritation, jealousy? How could it be jealousy, when she certainly had no designs on Mark herself? Oh, well. She had noticed that there seemed to be something going on between Dana and Mark. At least Dana seemed to be showing up a lot wherever Mark was, and the two talked frequently. Yet Dana was at least five years older than Mark. *But it's none of my business,* Julie reminded herself grudgingly.

Her mind wandered, and she came back to the present with a jolt as Rick dismissed the group. The man named Al gave them another breezy wave. She wondered who he was and why he was here. Maybe a Yale friend? Although he didn't look like her idea of a Yalie. She could hear her father scolding her for stereotyping.

"See you anon," Sandy said. "I'm off to rehearse the cast of *Six Who Pass While Lentils Boil.* Can you believe it?"

Julie laughed. "What is it? A play or a menu?"

"It's a play that Molly Hansen's mother starred in when she was a camper," Sandy explained, rolling her eyes. "It must have been around the time of the Civil War. Anyway, she sent Rick a copy with a request that we do it—Molly starring, naturally."

"And since Molly's family is loaded, Rick agreed."

"As Rick himself would say, you are an insightful human being. In other words, you're dead right," Sandy said with a wink, then took off with a group of children at her heels.

13

Joe shoved a piece of paper into Julie's hand as he passed her. Julie looked up to see a couple of girls watching and grinning, and she blushed. Joe was so unconcerned about what people thought. She loved getting all that attention from the big football star, but sometimes she wished he would be a bit more discreet. She unfolded the note slowly and read it. He had written, "Meet me out at the baseball field after Taps. PLEASE. If you don't, I'll kill myself. Love, Joe." Julie couldn't resist a smile. It was funny to think of Joe killing himself for love. He had tried before to lure her out to the ball field, but they weren't supposed to go very far from their cabins after Taps. Maybe one of these nights she'd take the chance, though. After all, Joe was a very attractive guy, and he was fun to be with.

Rick caught up with her. "Julie, if you don't mind, I thought Al and I would join you for the cookout. I have to keep my guest here properly entertained."

Al, standing with his hands in his hip pockets, looked amused. *He doesn't have a tan like the rest of us,* Julie thought; *that's one thing that makes him look different.*

"I'd love to have you," she said politely.

" 'Preciate it," Al drawled. He had pudgy cheeks and circles under his eyes. Either he was not in good health or he lived in a dungeon. He seemed like an odd man for Rick to have as a close friend, Julie thought. He was a person who smiled with his mouth but not

14

with his eyes. The eyes were watchful. Rick, on the other hand, gave the impression of smiling all over.

She went back to her cabin to keep an eye on the tidying up process. Pat especially liked to throw her Hudson Bay blanket over her unmade bed, hoping Julie wouldn't notice. And Jennifer had a way of leaving her toothpaste tube uncapped, with a thin red-and-white stream of paste oozing out, looking like a worm, as Mary said. Eleven- and twelve-year-olds could think up bizarre ideas.

The cabins were built in pairs, with a long, low bathroom and showers connecting them. There were two counselors and six girls to a cabin. The front wall of the cabin was screened in with bamboo curtains that could be rolled down in a storm. The outside wall was fitted with large windows, like the Assembly cabin, that could be latched open. There were four bunks along each wall, with Julie on one side, and Carol, her co-counselor, on the other.

The kids had arranged a row of trunks down the middle of the cabin to form a sort of wall. When Julie came into the cabin, Allie, the tall blond tennis player from California, was arguing with Jennifer as she struggled to retape her poster of The Talking Heads to the side of her trunk.

"I didn't knock it down on purpose," Jennifer contended. She was a healthy, rugged Montanan who could have posed for a cowgirl poster. "I can't help brushing against it when I open my trunk, can I?"

"You could be more careful." Allie's dark eyes looked stormy. "You do it on purpose. You don't like the Heads."

"I don't hate them that much. I just think they're flaky, that's all."

"They're not . . ." Allie's voice was rising.

"Hold it," Julie said. "It's too early in the day for warfare. Allie, I've got some strapping tape here somewhere; it might work better." She began to rummage through her trunk drawer.

Grumbling a little, Allie accepted the tape and forgot her anger. "I wish we had more wall space."

"Me too," piped up small, plump Mary. "I'd like to put up the blown-up picture Mom sent me of my cheerleading squad."

Pat's space was almost entirely taken up with a color photo of herself on the shore of Lake Como.

"It's Billie Jean's turn to sweep." Julie was looking at the list she kept.

Billie Jean, their one Texan, sprawled on her unmade bed. "I know, I know. I'm meditating."

"Not again," Allie said.

"Billie Jean meditates when there's something she doesn't want to do," Mary explained.

"It beats fighting," Billie Jean replied.

Pat strolled into the cabin.

"Make your bed, please, Pat," Julie said.

"I did." Pat batted innocent eyes at Julie.

"Pat, underneath as well as on top, okay?"

Pat sighed. "Julie, you're so strict."

"If you think Julie's strict," Billie Jean said, pulling herself together and getting the broom, "you ought to have Jackie Church."

"Or Dawn," said Regan. Regan was so shy she seldom said anything. "Dawn is a tyrant."

"Julie," Pat said, "is the best counselor in this camp."

Julie made a face but she was pleased. "Flattery will get you everywhere."

Pat grinned. "I know." She gave Julie a hug. "But I mean it."

"Sure enough, Julie is fair," Billie Jean said, "and she doesn't yell at us, although I wish she'd bring us some candy from town."

"I'll yell if you don't sweep around the trunks," Julie said, ignoring the comment about the forbidden candy. She surveyed the cabin, which was beginning to look less as if a tornado had struck it. "I've got to go see about extra food for the cookout. You guys finish up here, okay?"

Carol came in. "I'll ride herd on 'em, Julie." Julie nodded gratefully. Carol was a good counselor. The children liked her. One of her jobs was to play the bugle for Reveille, Assembly, meals, and Taps, and at flag-raising. She was good at it, and the silvery sound of her bugle was a familiar and pleasant part of camp

17

life. Rick played the bugle too, and once in a while they would station themselves at opposite ends of the camp, one bugle echoing the phrases of the other, at Taps. Julie loved it; it brought tears to her eyes, it was so beautiful.

"Are you taking Dana's morning class?" Carol asked Julie.

"No, she didn't want me to. She's got some program going that she wants to stay with. So I've got some free time."

Julie started for the Hash House. On a clear day like this one, she liked the walk from one side of the camp to the other. The Bitter Root camp grounds curved around the southern end of the lake. The tennis courts, archery range, and Rick's cabin were behind her as she walked along past the girls' cabins. The Assembly cabin lay ahead, looking out over the lake at the point where the bottom part of the U began. There was a slight rise in the land beside it, just before the ground sloped down to the cove where the swimming area, dock, and boats were.

As she skirted that part, she stopped for a minute to watch Dana working with the five-to-eights, both boys and girls. One child stood at the end of the dock, bent over, arms extended and fingertips together, trying to get up the nerve to dive. Dana was talking to her, patting her stomach, trying to get the little girl to straighten her knees. Julie laughed. She could remember her own initial terror of diving, back when her father first taught her to swim at their summer cottage on Flathead Lake. But she had mastered it in time, and now she loved diving. An eight-year-old named Aaron, who was going on the outing in the afternoon, was trying to show another boy how to float. Already an excellent swimmer, Aaron seemed to be enjoying his role as instructor. Some of the children saw Julie and waved and yelled and did a few fancy tricks for her benefit. The child on the end of the dock was so unnerved by the shouting that she fell forward into the lake in a belly-flop.

"Ouch!" Julie said, cringing. Quickly, she waved and moved on before she disrupted Dana's class altogether.

On the other side of the U, sloping up away from the shore, was the Hash House, the low, rambling dining room and kitchen where Mrs. O'Reilly reigned. Mrs. O'Reilly was the nutritionist responsible for the excellent meals prepared by the two graduate students who were cooks that summer.

Beyond the Hash House were the office, the nurse's bungalow, a small store that sold cookies, Granola bars, raisins, fruit juices, and stamps. Beyond that the boys' cabins spread out in a pie-shaped formation among the pine trees. The parking space was beside the Hash House, and the private road that connected with the county road began here. Back of the Hash House were the basketball and volleyball courts. Further along the road was the ball field.

As she went into the kitchen, Julie was mentally counting out ears of corn, hamburger patties, buns. It felt good to be in charge of something, entirely on her own, and she was pleased that Dana had given her this job. She wanted to be sure it went well, though. How much, for instance, would a man like Al what's-his-name eat? He looked greedy, a man of many starches. His stomach hung over his belt.

Mark was just coming out of the Hash House with a cup of coffee in his hand, looking handsome in his hiking shorts and his blue-and-white Yale T-shirt. He smiled at her, and she got the shock she always felt when those intensely blue eyes turned her way.

"Any special requests in the way of food?" she asked, hoping she sounded casual.

"Just plenty of it," Mark replied. "Our lives are in your hands."

She tried desperately to think of a witty reply but could only come up with, "I'll try to live up to it."

"You will." And then he was gone, a flock of children suddenly materializing to trail at his heels like sparrows.

Later she knew she would think of a whole bunch of brilliant remarks. She wished she could be more re-laxed so she'd think of a good reply in time to say it. When she wanted to shine most, she was quiet. Her mom said she'd outgrow it, assured her that it was a question of self-confidence. Whatever it was a question of, she'd flunked it again, Julie thought despairingly. But she shouldn't be trying to impress Mark anyway. Dana had first dibs on him.

She went into the warm, good-smelling kitchen thinking, "Pickles. Don't forget the pickles."

Chapter 2

Fortunately, the trip up the lake went smoothly. The kids took their responsibility seriously, and there was no reckless horsing around in the canoes.

The weather was perfect, the lake still and brilliant in the western light. On the other shore they could see a few boats near the scattered summer cottages, a catamaran, an outboard with a man fishing in a cove, a sailboat with vivid red sails. A man and woman in an inboard passed near them and waved. Their voices carried across the water as the man said, "They're from the camp," and the woman answered, "They look so little." The wash from their boat gently rocked the canoes.

"Little!" Pat snorted, obviously offended. She was

paddling stern in the canoe where Julie was a passenger.

When they arrived at the beach where the cookout was to be, the children helped Julie unload her baskets of food. As far as she could see, she had not forgotten anything, although she had almost neglected to put in the matches until Dana had reminded her.

The children stripped down to their swimsuits and shrieked and jumped around in the cold water. Here in the shadow of Bear Mountain, the water was colder than it was at camp. Julie swam briefly and then set about getting things ready. She detailed several children, including Pat and Ham, to collect wood for the fire.

She wished Mark and his group would come. The children had explored the woods near the beach and now they were showing signs of getting restless. She had to break up a sand-throwing game and then persuade Aaron and another little boy to come out of the water before they turned blue.

"You, Ham," she called, as Ham was heading for the woods again, "stick around."

"More wood," he yelled.

"We've got enough for now," Julie called back. She was a little nervous because Ham had been teasing Pat, daring her to go up the mountain to the tarn, the small icy-cold lake in a hollow of rocks near the top of the mountain. She didn't want them venturing far into the woods and especially not up to the tarn. This was not called Bear Mountain for nothing. On the other hand, she didn't want to frighten them unnecessarily. Rick's philosophy was to make campers aware of the potential dangers of the wilderness without making them panicky. That, Julie thought, was more easily said than done.

Ham and Pat joined some of the other children who were hanging around Julie, offering to help yet mostly just getting in the way. She was patient, though, trying to assign small chores to them that would make them feel useful.

"Will you open the jars of pickles, Ham?" Julie asked, handing him the opener.

"Pat's afraid to go up to the tarn," Ham announced, ignoring his counselor. He ducked as Pat aimed a fist at him.

"I am not," she retorted.

"Scaredy-cat, scaredy-cat," he taunted, dancing around her just out of reach.

"Ham!" Julie said threateningly. "Pay attention to the pickles. Nobody is going up to the tarn."

"Why not?" Jennifer asked, sneaking a potato chip from the big wooden bowl that Julie had meant to place out of reach until dinner.

"I don't even know what a tarn is," Pat said. "And I could care less."

"It's a small, little pool," Ham said, "in this kind of hollow, with these big huge rocks all around it."

"How do you know?" Pat asked.

25

"I went up there last summer, a bunch of us on a hike. It wasn't Mark, though; he wasn't here then."

"We all know that," Pat said loftily. She brushed sand off her new white shorts.

"It's bottomless." Ham was still trying to get Pat's attention.

"Nothing is bottomless," Mary told him. "Right, Julie?"

Julie saw that Ham was beginning to look beleaguered. She didn't want to embarrass him. "I guess when we say bottomless, we mean very, very deep. Ham's right about that."

"It sounds mysterious," Jennifer said, pulling on her braids excitedly. "I wish we could see it."

"I could show you," Ham began, but Julie cut him short.

"Ham, nobody, but nobody, is going near the tarn. Understood?" Her tone of voice meant business, and the campers knew it.

He gave her his quick grin. "Yeah, okay." But he couldn't resist adding, "There's a cave, too. Nobody knows about it but me."

"Oh, you know so much," Pat said. "Little boys think they know everything."

Julie saw the flash of hurt that crossed Ham's face. She started to say something to distract them, but at that moment there was a shout, and Mark and his group came running down the narrow fire trail from the mountain. They had climbed an adjoining trail on

Thorne Mountain and come over to Bear Mountain on a high switchback. They looked hot and tired and happy. Julie was very glad to see them.

The campers immediately headed for the cool water, and Mark had to restrain some of them from plunging in with their clothes on. "You'd freeze when the sun goes down," he told them. "Get your suits." Feeling relieved and suddenly hungry, Julie started the fire. Looking over the pile, she realized they might not have enough wood yet. "Ham, we do need a little more wood. Why don't you take some buddies along and scout it out. Remember, dry wood. Look for deadfalls."

Somebody shouted and pointed toward the lake. Rick's boat had come into sight, and the putt-putt of the motor reached them faintly. Julie wished they weren't coming. It would have been nicer if just she and Mark were there. The boat's approach made her all the more nervous about how things were going. "I wish I'd started the potatoes sooner," she muttered.

Mark had come out of the lake and joined her. He heard what she said. "It'll be okay. Rick isn't the Great Pooh-Bah, after all. He can wait for his food like the rest of us."

She laughed.

"What can I do to help?" he said.

"Maybe get the water boiling for the corn?"

He set up the heavy kettle.

"Did you have a good climb?" she asked, trying not

27

to think about how terrific he looked in swim trunks. Standing this close to Mark, she could forget how to boil water.

"Real good. The kids were great. Sometimes I have to get tough with them, but not today." His long eyelashes were stuck together from swimming, and his dark hair was curling up in little ringlets. She noticed he had goosebumps on his tanned arms, and for a moment she felt tempted to rub his arms the way she did with her youngest campers when they came out of the lake blue-lipped and shivering.

"Your trip go all right?" Mark asked, breaking into her reverie.

"Fine. They were serious and pleased with themselves. But I'm glad you got here. They were beginning to get antsy."

Mark picked up his knapsack and went to change his clothes as Ham brought over an armful of wood. He was still teasing Pat, and she made brief lunges at him from time to time, as if to get revenge. It was obvious that he loved it. But Julie quickly forgot about Pat and Ham as Rick's boat came into the cove. *Don't get nervous,* she told herself, *everything's going fine*.

Taking some of the hamburgers out of the cooler, Julie arranged them on the long-handled grill that Mrs. O'Reilly had loaned her. She handed the shucked ears of corn to Mark to put in the kettle of boiling water. Pickles, potato chips, rolls, relish . . . Mentally she counted off the list and found what she needed. Paper

28

plates. Dixie cups. She glanced up at the sky—it had gotten cloudy.

Mary and another camper came and hung over her shoulder as she unpacked. "I'm starving," Mary declared. She helped herself to a handful of chips.

"Look, you guys," Julie said. "If you want to eat, leave me room." She straightened up and counted noses. "Where are Pat and Ham?"

"Pat chased Ham into the woods," Mark said as he rejoined them. "Don't worry, they'll come back as soon as they smell the food. Ham especially; you can count on it."

Rick had brought his guitar and the children were begging him to play. "After we eat," he promised. He had overheard Mark's comment about Pat and Ham. "I don't like having the kids in the woods," he said, looking at Julie. "I'm sure it's safe, but you never know. Al and I will go and look for them."

He said it pleasantly, but Julie felt rebuked. She should have been keeping track. But it was hard to concentrate on all the details of the picnic and still keep track of every kid!

"They're probably clear to the tarn by now." Allie spoke up, practicing imaginary serves with an imaginary racquet.

"They wouldn't do that," Julie said, horrified. She knew Ham was adventurous, and Pat too, but she didn't think they would deliberately disobey her. Still, she was glad Rick and Al had gone to look. With Rick here she couldn't concentrate on the cooking. She checked the potatoes. They weren't done yet, but they were getting there. The corn would need ten minutes or so. That gave her time for all the little things. Mark had spread a plastic cloth over the ground and unwrapped the utensils. She found a platter of onions he'd sliced and looked over at him. He was a fast worker. Wishing they had a picnic table, she began arranging potato chips, rolls, condiments, and the plates.

Mark turned the hamburgers on the grill. They were starting to smell wonderful. Julie's stomach growled and she looked around to see if Pat and Ham were back yet. They weren't. She didn't want to start serving before Rick and Al got back, but they were taking a long time to find two kids. A shower of sand hit her leg.

"Aaron, please! Don't kick sand in the food."

Aaron was one of the kids in Joe's cabin. He tended to get into trouble. When it became apparent that he was going to ignore Julie, Mark came over and draped a friendly arm around Aaron, steering him away from the food. *He handles kids a lot better than I do,* Julie thought.

Ten minutes later, everything was ready to serve, and she was hot and anxious. Where was Rick?

Just then Ham and Pat came down the path. He was holding her hand, but he dropped it as they came into view. Julie was surprised that Pat let him hold her hand. She glanced at Pat again. The child looked upset. Had they had a fight or something? But the children were lining up for supper, and she had no time to think about Pat just then.

Mark helped her serve the food. He was certainly being sweet and helpful. But she wished Rick would come back. She wasn't about to try and hold off this hungry crowd any longer. She hoped he wouldn't be mad.

"Where did you guys disappear to?" Mark asked Ham.

"Just up there." Ham's usual loquaciousness seemed to have vanished. The next time she looked up, Pat and Ham were sitting together apart from the group. They had big plates of food but Pat wasn't eating.

As soon as she could, Julie went over to her. "What's the matter, Pat?"

"Nothing."

"You aren't eating."

"She has a stomach-ache," Ham said defensively. He looked anxious. There was a crackling of twigs in the underbrush and Rick and Al appeared. They both looked disheveled, especially Al. Rick, however, looked very relieved when he saw Pat and Ham, and came over to where they sat. "We looked all over for you kids. You shouldn't go off like that."

Moonstone

Neither child answered him.

"Something wrong, Pat?" He stood looking down at her.

She shook her head and continued to stare at his leather cowboy boots.

"She has a stomach-ache," Julie said.

Rick nodded. "I see. Well, I bet you got into the blueberry patch up there. We noticed somebody had been feasting, but I thought it might have been bears."

"Bears?" Pat looked frightened.

"Yes, that's why you shouldn't wander around up there," Rick said, giving her a pat on the head.

"Hey, Julie, that food smells wonderful. Tuck some of those good vitamins under your belt, Pat—you'll feel better."

Pat didn't say anything.

Julie thought Ham looked pale, too. Probably they had both eaten too many blueberries.

When the last child had been fed, Julie took her own plate away from the group and sat down on the sand with her back against one of the overturned canoes. She was tired but pleased with the way things had gone. Except for Pat's tummy-ache. She'd give her some antacid pills from the dispensary shelf when they got back. From where she sat, she couldn't see Ham and Pat, but probably they were recovered now. Eating solid food would help them to feel better. Poor, love-struck Ham.

After a little while, Rick got out his guitar and scooted up to sit near the fire. The children quickly surrounded him. Julie glanced at the sky. It was getting dark too soon; rain clouds were piling up. *Hold off till we get home,* she thought. It wouldn't do to paddle home in a storm—the lake could get rough very fast. But maybe the storm would circle around them. She hoped Rick was keeping track of the weather.

Julie closed her eyes and leaned back comfortably, listening to the pleasant sound of the guitar. Rick would sing first, then the children would join in. The piney scent of the air and the light breeze was a delightful combination. She began to feel very relaxed and content.

Suddenly she sat up. She had dozed off—how embarrassing! Had Rick noticed? No, he was still singing. But the evening had darkened still more, which made her uneasy. She didn't want to be responsible for all those kids in canoes if it got really dark. She wished she had her father's knack for telling whether it was going to storm or not.

Mark was busy putting more wood on the fire. For a moment he seemed to be outlined in flame. Then the blaze died down and he took on his usual shape: tall, small-waisted, broad-shouldered, long-legged. A very satisfactory shape. Julie closed her eyes again, listening to the music and the sound of the water against the sand. Once she thought she heard the faint sound of far-off thunder. They really ought to start home. But Rick didn't take too kindly to suggestions from the staff about what should be done. If a storm really did break, he'd have to take the kids home in several trips in the motorboat and leave the canoes to be picked up later. She wasn't going to interfere, but she wouldn't agree to a risky trip back to camp, either.

She jumped as someone plunked down beside her. It was Al.

"Quite a bunch of kids," he said.

She wasn't sure what that meant and replied, "They're great kids."

"Ruined my shoes climbing on that stupid mountain." He leaned over and rubbed one of the brown suede shoes.

"City shoes," Julie observed.

"Right. I didn't know I was going to make like a mountain goat."

Carefully she moved a few inches away from him. He smelled of shaving lotion, and it was not her favorite brand.

"Don't know much about kids myself," he said, lighting a cigarette and blowing the smoke in her direction. "You from these parts?"

"Yes. I live in Whitefish."

"Whitefish. I gotta hand you Montanans the trophy for thinking up weird names."

She wanted to say there was nothing weird about Whitefish.

34

"And where'd they get a crazy name like Bitter Root?"

"The bitter root is the state flower," Julie said. "And there's a valley near Missoula called the Bitter Root Valley."

"Missoula!" he chuckled. "Weird."

Trying not to sound defensive, Julie asked, "Where are you from?"

"Me? The Coast."

That was hardly a forthcoming answer, but she wasn't interested in pursuing the subject. He probably lived in Los Angeles. She listened to the song the children were singing. It was an old Army song, "When the Caissons Go Rolling Along," but some past camper or counselor had changed the words to ". . . so it's heigh heigh ho, you will always know, when Camp Bitter Root comes swinging along." Bitter Root didn't fit the beat, but they managed it.

"What does your father do?" Al asked her.

"My father?" That was a weird question. Maybe he was trying to make polite conversation. "He's district attorney."

"Is that right?" Al sounded amused.

She'd had enough of Al. She got to her feet. "Excuse me. I have to see about the children."

"Sure thing."

From the corner of her eye, Julie saw Ham coming out of the woods as if he were trying not to be noticed. What kind of game was he playing? She ought to scold him; it would be dark in the woods now and he shouldn't be running around up there. Julie walked over to meet him. "Ham, where's Pat?"

"Pat?" He sounded as if he'd never heard of anyone named Pat.

"I don't see her."

"She . . . uh . . . had to go to the bathroom. She'll be back."

"Does she feel better?"

"Better? Oh yeah."

Julie felt exasperated. No one could be so uncommunicative as a small boy. She thought he looked as if he had been running. He was breathing hard, and his forehead had drops of perspiration on it. How worked up did a nine-year-old boy get about love, anyway? She tried to remember. Probably they'd just been chasing each other, playing games.

Ham brushed past her, and she saw Mark go to him. She watched as he drew the boy aside to talk. She couldn't hear what they were saying, but Ham kept shaking his head. When she joined them, Ham sidled away.

"Ham says Pat is in the woods," she said.

"I know." Mark sounded grim.

His tone alarmed her. "I guess I should go and find her."

"I don't know what's with those kids," he said, running his hand through his hair distractedly. "Ham doesn't usually act crazy."

"Neither does Pat," Julie agreed. "I'm going to look for her."

Mark paused, then said, "Okay, I'm coming with you."

She wondered if he blamed her for not keeping closer watch. She felt defensive. But he obviously hadn't noticed the kids' absence either. There were twenty-two kids at the cookout, after all.

Mark went ahead of her, unsnapping a flashlight from his belt. It was quite dark as soon as they got into the trees. "Pat needs some discipline," he said.

"She's not all that bad," Julie defended her camper. She didn't like to hear Pat criticized, especially since she *was* a good kid. If anything happened to her . . . Julie shivered and tried to put the disturbing thought out of her head. The growing darkness that had made sitting around the campfire so cozy suddenly seemed malevolent and threatening now that she was away from the group. Julie ran to catch up with Mark's bobbing light. Darn him. Why was he going so fast?

As the path widened, she caught up with him. She kept calling Pat's name, but there was no answer. Suddenly she tripped over an exposed root. Pain shot through her leg, and she cried out.

Mark caught her arm. "You okay?"

"I only broke my toe in twenty places, that's all," Julie snapped. The touch of his hand on her arm disturbed her.

"You're kidding, I hope."

Julie glared at him, then remembered he couldn't see her face in the dark.

"I guess. But it hurts." She moved on, calling Pat's name again. There was no answer. "We've got to be careful, you know; there are bears in these woods."

"And a wolverine, possibly, and coyotes, and who knows what. The great American West."

He sounded so contemptuous she wanted to shout, "No one forced you to come here." But instead she replied, "Coyotes don't attack people, and wolverines won't let you get within a mile of them."

He didn't answer. She wondered if it was because he felt as worried as she did, and that made him sound cross, or because he didn't care. She hoped it wasn't the latter. They stopped to examine a place where bushes had been trampled. But the brush on each side of the trail here was too thick for anyone to have gone off the path without leaving signs.

Toward the top of the mountain, it would still be light. If Pat had wandered up far enough, she wouldn't realize that it was so dark farther down.

The path narrowed. Branches reached out like clutching hands, scratching her face and arms. She tripped and half fell into some prickly bushes. Trees reared up in front of her like monsters waiting to pounce. She couldn't bear to think of Pat up here alone, perhaps sick.

Then Mark's light went out, and darkness fell on them like a huge cape. He didn't say anything for a moment, and Julie realized she was trembling. "Light's gone," he finally said. He turned to go back. "We'll have to get Rick's."

The pale blur of his shirt was the only guide she had. She had to hurry to keep up with him. Going downhill fast made her knees feel weak. She wanted to say, "Slow down!" but at the same time, there was a sense of urgency driving her that wouldn't allow it. Pat *had* to be found.

When she stumbled into the clearing, Mark was already talking to Rick. Rick turned to her, looking concerned.

"We'll find her, don't worry. We have to find her." His ever-present smile was gone. "Al and I will search. Julie, you and Mark take the kids home."

"It looks like a storm coming up," Julie said.

Rick glanced up. "Oh, I don't think we'll get it."

She wished she could be so sure. The lake looked black.

Rick was calling the children together, forcing a cheerful tone. "Time to go, kids. End of a perfect day. Everybody into the canoes. Aaron, you and Mary go in Julie's canoe—you too, Mason. Allie, take two of the younger ones in Mark's canoe . . ." He went on, efficiently assigning places. In a low voice he said to Julie, "Don't mention Pat to the kids."

"I'll stay and help search," Mark said.

"No, you won't. Thanks, Mark, but if Al and I are late, nobody will notice. If you were, they'd wonder."

"They'll wonder anyway about Pat."

Rick took Mark's arm and moved him away where he could speak to him without being overheard. Julie could tell they were arguing. She wondered why Mark wanted so much to stay.

Rick won, of course. But as Mark strode over to the canoes and began to hurry the children, Julie noticed that his flashlight was working again. How strange! Maybe it wasn't the same flashlight. She looked more closely. No, it was the same one. Had Mark been lying when he said it didn't work anymore? But she couldn't think of any reason why he would. She walked over to where he stood. "Your light's working," she said.

"Ham borrowed it and wore down the battery. Sometimes it comes back on if you shake it." He sounded abrupt.

"If the kids ask, Julie," Rick said, coming up from behind her, "say Pat wasn't feeling well and we took her across the lake to Vinegar Cove to see the doctor."

The trip back to camp was horrible. Julie was very nervous; she was worried about Pat, and she was worried about the weather. The sky was almost as dark as night now, and the thunder was ominously close. Lightning flashed jagged patterns over the mountains. Some of the younger children grew quite frightened. She clenched her teeth as the canoe plowed through the water. Without saying anything, she and Mark had herded the canoes into a tight pattern. At one point Regan's canoe almost hit one of the others.

"Watch it!" Mark said.

"We can't see—it's too dark," Aaron said, sounding tense.

"Nonsense," Julie replied, more sharply than she meant to. "We're doing fine." Softening her tone, she added, "We'll be home in a few minutes."

A sudden streak of lightning split the dark ahead of them. It was followed by an earsplitting clap of thunder that all but drowned out the children's shrieks. And then, as suddenly as if someone had overturned a cosmic bucket, the rain came in a downpour. Julie flinched as the cold drops ran down her neck and back, and clenching her teeth, she tried to put still more strength into her stroke. Luckily they were not far from camp now.

The younger children huddled against the rain. Glancing at the other canoes, Julie felt proud of the way her campers were handling the task of getting the canoes safely to shore. She must remember to congratulate them later.

When her own canoe pulled alongside the dock at last, Ham was already there. He reached for the bow and held it steady while they got out. Even though he was drenched and shivering, he helped Julie put the canoes up on the rack. But when she turned to thank him, he was gone.

"Everybody into a hot shower and to bed," she

called above the noise of the rain. She saw Mark, his hair plastered flat and dripping, heave his canoe onto the rack and leave with some of the boys skittering along close at his heels.

Well, they had made it. All but Pat.

Back in the cabin, Jennifer asked, "Where's Pat?"

Julie paused only a split second before answering, "She wasn't feeling well. She's coming back with Rick."

"Oh, the lucky duck. I wish I could ride in Rick's boat." Not trusting herself to reply, Julie turned her attention to getting everybody ready for bed. When Carol came up to her a little later to ask if everything was all right, Julie forced herself to nod. "It's okay."

She wished she could believe her own words. Pat's absence was like an aching space inside herself. Even after she shucked off her wet things and changed into dry clothes, she didn't feel any better. She couldn't stop thinking that if she had paid closer attention, Pat wouldn't be missing. What if she had had an attack of appendicitis? She wondered if Rick would be able to get hold of Pat's father if anything bad had happened. Pat had said he'd be "out of this world" for a week, and then he would call her from Nairobi when he got out of the jungle.

After the girls had finally quieted down and gone to bed, she lay tensely on her cot, still dressed, listening for the sound of Rick's boat.

After a little while, Allie began talking in her sleep,

having a nightmare. Grateful for something to do since she was so wide awake, Julie got up quietly and sat beside her, holding her hand till she half woke, then went back to sleep peacefully. Allie's parents were in the midst of getting a divorce, and she was unhappy over it. How lucky I am to have parents that like each other so much, Julie thought. The three of them had always done things together as a family, whether it was fishing for salmon in Washington or struggling with the *New York Times* crossword puzzle.

Gradually, Julie became aware that the thunder and lightning had passed off to the east and the rain had slowed to a steady rhythm. Suddenly she couldn't stand it any longer—she had to go see if there was any news of Pat. Rick could have come in and she might not have heard him during the hubbub that went on when the kids were getting ready for bed. Putting on her slicker, Julie walked down to the beach.

It was hard to see, but as she got near the dock she saw someone sitting on the diving board, staring out into the darkness of the lake. Coming closer, she saw that it was Mark. He had not heard her. He lifted his arm and peered at his watch, almost impatiently, as if he were waiting for someone.

"Mark?"

He jumped violently, as if she had shouted. Then he slid off the board. "You startled me." He sounded accusing.

"I'm sorry. The rain makes so much noise," she

said, trying to defend herself. What right had he to jump on her like that?

Mark seemed appeased. "Yeah, okay."

"No sign of Rick?"

"No."

"Did Ham tell you any more?"

"He's clammed up tight. Sticks to his story."

"He seemed frightened, I thought."

"Well, he's devoted to Pat." Mark glanced at his watch again and then edged away as if he didn't want to talk to her.

She wanted to keep him there, find out what he was thinking, what he was doing there. He was the only one she could talk to about it. Without knowing why the thought had come into her head, she said, "Did you know Rick very well at college? I mean were you friends?"

Mark gave her a strange look. He was frowning. "He taught a section of English that I took, that's all."

Julie hesitated. She wanted to ask more questions, but Mark's face didn't encourage her to cross-examine him.

"Why?" he said. "Why'd you ask me that?"

Julie took a step backwards. "I . . . I don't know. I was just thinking it must be very hard on Rick, having something like this happen. I was wondering how he'd react. Everything's gone so smoothly all summer."

Mark didn't answer. In a minute he said, "There's

no use staying here in the rain. I'll see you in the morning."

The night swallowed him up abruptly, leaving Julie with the eerie feeling that their conversation had been some sort of ghostly encounter. She shivered and pulled her sweater around her. She had the distinct impression that Mark wasn't saying what he really thought, and she wondered why. He seemed almost hostile.

Her mind went back to Pat on the mountain. She thought of wolverines and shuddered. What she had told Mark was true; a wolverine would do everything in his power to stay away if he knew in advance you were coming. But once she had surprised one in a cave, and the wolverine had scratched her arm as he shot past her trying to get out. It wasn't an attack; the animal had just panicked. Her parents had asked Dr. Prier to give her tetanus shots, though. The Indians called the wolverine "carcajou," and they believed an evil spirit lived in the animal. They never killed wolverines.

She tensed, thinking she heard the throb of a motor. A few seconds later she was sure. They were coming back—they had found Pat! She felt an immense wave of relief. Everything was going to be all right. She slid off the diving board and stood at the end of the dock, listening to the tiny beat of sound grow stronger. The rain had turned to a drizzle; a breeze had come up, and waves were slapping against the pilings.

Soon she saw the dark shape of the boat. Now that her worst fears were melting away, she could laugh at herself for getting into such a state.

The light from the boat swept a little to the left of her as Rick brought it into the cove and cut the motor for docking. She strained her eyes to see Pat's small outline, but all she could see was Rick. As he came alongside in the sudden silence, she caught her breath in alarm.

There was no one in the boat but Rick.

Chapter 3

Before Rick was out of the boat, Julie cried out, "Where's Pat?"

Wearily, he got out and began tying up the boat. She watched him, waiting for his answer, feeling cold in her stomach.

"Julie . . ." He turned to her finally and put his arm around her shoulders. "We haven't found her. Yet. But I haven't given up hope."

"Give up hope? She *has* to be out there. She couldn't just vanish."

"Of course she couldn't." His voice reminded her of old Dr. Ellis's when he told her grandmother she was going to be just fine, even though he knew good and well she was going to die.

"Joe's over there, looking."

"Joe?"

"Yes. I came and got him. He knows this country extremely well. I'm back now because I have to check up, but I'll be out there at the first crack of dawn. Don't worry, she's there, and Joe and Al will find her. They've got blankets and food and a Coleman lantern."

She hoped it would be Joe and not Al who found Pat. Al didn't seem like a fountain of comfort for a frightened child. But Rick seemed to grow more and more convinced, as they talked, that everything would turn out all right. She would just have to trust him.

"We don't want to alarm the children," he continued. "So I'll ask Meredith to take over Assembly and tell the kids Pat wasn't feeling well, which is true, and that we've taken her to the doctor, which we'll certainly do as soon as we find her." Rick was silent for a moment as he looked out over the lake. Then in a different voice, almost as if he were talking to himself, he said, "It isn't like Pat to get sick and go off alone. She's a gregarious kid."

Julie didn't say so but she thought it *was* like Pat. She wanted people to see her as poised and confident. She was used to solving her own problems, and like a cat she would go off alone if she felt ill.

A little while later, back in bed, Julie lay awake a long time, trying not to imagine how scared Pat must be, alone on the dark and stormy mountain. She thought of the varnished wooden signs on mountain trails, put there by the Forest Service. In her mind's eye she saw letters burned into the wood that warned: "Grizzly territory. Leave no food. No perfume, deodorant, or scent of any kind. Make noise to alert bears to your presence." When she and her father hiked in grizzly country, they wore bear bells on their legs.

At last she slept. But her dreams were not peaceful. Instead, she dreamed she was standing above the tarn, staring down into the black, deep, killing-cold beneath her. She felt herself falling . . . falling forward and down . . . falling, falling . . .

She woke up with a lurch of terror, and it took a minute for her to realize it had been only a dream. The rain had stopped and the sun was rising in the east. As Julie lay there, listening, she heard the sound of Rick's boat leaving. She stared into the dripping clump of birches outside the cabin. Of course Pat would be found, scared but all right. Rick was doing all he could. She had to be out there somewhere; a child didn't just evaporate. Julie went back to sleep.

Just before Carol went off to play Reveille, Julie heard the boat again. Quickly she got dressed and went down to the beach. Rick and Mark were standing on the dock deep in conversation. Both of them looked shaken. As she approached, Mark started to say something, then bit his lip and hurriedly walked away. Her heart began to pound.

"Did you find her?"

Rick seemed to have trouble speaking, Rick who had always been so at ease. "It's bad news, Julie."

She tried to speak, but her throat seemed to close up.

"Joe went up to . . ." He took a deep breath. There was a rip in his shirt sleeve. "Joe went up to the tarn, and when I got there we both went up. Pat's white sweater was on the rocks close to the tarn."

Julie closed her eyes. That white cashmere sweater was one of Pat's favorites. It would be like her to take it off if she were scrambling around those jagged rocks. And if Pat had fallen in, Julie knew, there was practically no chance that she could have survived. The water in the tarn was icy cold and very deep, like Yellowstone Lake, so that a person would be paralyzed in a couple of minutes.

"If she fell into the tarn, she would die," Julie said. Her voice sounded hollow.

Rick turned his face away. His Adam's apple jerked.

"Where is the sweater?"

"I left it. Search and Rescue doesn't like to have things touched."

"You called Search and Rescue?"

He nodded. "They're up there now." He ran his hand over his hair. "I can't even get in touch with her father for another week." He turned to Julie. "But if the kids find out, it will ruin the camp."

Julie was shocked. How could he worry about a

thing like that right now? But, after thinking about it for a moment, she understood his thinking. He was responsible for the camp, after all. There would certainly be a panic, parents coming to snatch their kids to safety, possibly lawsuits. "I see what you mean."

"I knew you would."

A sob choked her. "It's so awful. That terrific kid . . ."

He put his arm around her. "Stiff upper lip, Julie. We haven't given up yet."

She leaned against him for a moment, taking some comfort from his strength, and grateful that he wasn't blaming her for Pat's disappearance.

"I'm counting on you. For the good of the camp," Rick said. He patted her shoulder and walked away.

The notes of Reveille rang out over the sleeping camp. Julie knew she ought to get back to the cabin, but she lingered a little longer, trying to get herself together. In spite of what Rick had said, in spite of the evidence of the sweater, she could not really accept the idea that Pat had drowned. Something tugged at her mind that she couldn't get hold of.

Mentally, she tried to retrace Pat's steps. She had gone into the woods, Ham said. She was not feeling well. And then for some unimaginable reason, even though it was getting dark, she must have climbed that steep trail halfway up the mountain to the tarn. Had Ham, in spite of what he had said, gone with her? Was

51

it a lark that turned tragic? He'd been dying to show off his knowledge of the tarn. But surely if Pat had fallen in, no matter how frightened he was, he would have come running back to tell them. She saw the tarn in her mind—she'd been up there in her camper days—it was beautiful, black, and menacing, not a place where kids would linger.

When she got back to the cabin she was greeted with a buzz of questions about Pat. Where was she? Did she feel better? Had she been lost?

"We'll find out at Assembly," Julie said, hoping she sounded reassuring. "She had a stomach-ache last night."

The girls began imagining all kinds of horrible fates for Pat. Julie knew they weren't serious, but still it was hard for her to listen to them. When Billie Jean got to the point of having Pat eaten by a bear, Julie stopped them.

Her campers looked over at her in surprise, and Allie came over and gave Julie a hug. "We're only kidding. We know she's okay."

"What little ghouls they are," Carol commented as she and Julie walked toward the Hash House after flag-raising and mess call. Carol was short and plump with braces on her teeth. Next year she would be a first-year student at Northern Montana College in Havre, aiming for a career as a geologist. She was dependable and easygoing, and Julie had grown fond of her. She desperately wished she could talk to her co-counselor about what Rick had told her.

The girls and boys lined up on the wide steps of the Hash House for the song they sang every morning:

Here we stand like birds in the wilderness,
Birds in the wilderness, birds in the wilderness,
Here we stand like birds in the wilderness,
Waiting for our food.

Rick was not at breakfast, and neither was Joe. Instead, Meredith sat in Rick's place at the head table. When the food arrived, Julie realized she had no appetite. Looking around the dining room, she saw Mark across the room and tried to catch his eye, but he seemed to be avoiding looking at her. Ham was not there, either. Ham, who was noted for his appetite, missing a meal? But she wasn't going to worry, she reminded herself, not too much anyway. Search and Rescue would find Pat. They were very thorough.

On the way out of the dining room Mark caught up with her and said, "Rick wants to see you in the Counselors' Room."

Startled, she asked, "What for?"

He shook his head and walked away. She wondered if he was blaming her for Pat's disappearance. He had been there too, after all. But, she reminded herself, it was officially your cookout. You were the one in charge.

She wondered, too, why Rick had sent Mark to tell her to come. Sometimes the two of them seemed distant with each other, yet at other times they acted almost as if they shared secrets. She thought of Mark looking at his watch and waiting in the rain.

Sandy caught up with her. "What's up?"

"I'm not sure. Mark says Rick wants to see me."

"Why's he picking on you? Mark was there too. So was Rick, for that matter. The kid's all right, isn't she? It's not your fault she got sick," Sandy pointed out.

"I don't think he's picking on me," Julie replied. But her friend's words made her uneasy. They echoed her own thoughts.

Sandy wanted to ask her other questions, but Julie shook her head. "I can't talk about it right now, okay? I'll see you later." When she arrived at the Counselors' Room, Rick and Mark were already there, deep in conversation. They stopped when she came in.

Al joined them. He looked no different, except perhaps a little more poker-faced. Doesn't his expression ever change? Julie wondered. She glanced at his shoes and saw that they were dirty and scarred. So he really had been climbing around on the mountain. It surprised her that he would care enough about a lost child to go to all that trouble.

Rick got right down to business. "Julie, please tell

me everything you remember about Pat's movements, where she went, what she said, what she did, everything," he demanded, leaning against the cabin wall with his arms crossed.

She was startled. He sounded almost accusing, as if there were something she hadn't told him. But probably he was just tense. Carefully she repeated all that she could remember. Rick took notes.

He glanced at Al. "The stories jibe."

"What stories?" When he didn't answer, she began to feel a little indignant. "You were all there too," she said accusingly, looking around at the three faces.

"You were in charge of the kids, Julie," Rick replied.

She couldn't believe it. Was he going to make her the fall guy? *Don't be paranoid,* she told herself. He's just worried. It makes him sound stern, that's all. She looked back at Mark, standing by the door with his arms folded. His blue eyes looked remote, as if he didn't know her. *"You* were there too," she said to him.

When he didn't answer, tears sprang to her eyes. "I don't believe she's in that tarn. Pat had too much sense." As soon as she said the words, she realized she had been feeling that way all along.

"If she was climbing around those rocks, and not feeling good," Al maintained, "anything could happen."

"I don't believe she would go up there."

"Then where is she?" Rick broke in, sounding really upset.

Julie had never seen him like this. He'd always been so in control before, so smiling.

"All right, listen. Meredith will make an announcement to the kids that Pat was ill," he said. "She'll tell them that we've taken her to the hospital. Otherwise we'd have wholesale panic, and parents pouring in here. Thank God the owners are in Europe. Please remember . . ." He looked hard at both Julie and Mark. "The camp morale—in fact, the whole future of this place—depends on you people."

Much as Julie hated the idea of lying to the kids, she realized she didn't have a choice. She surprised herself, though, by asking, "Have you notified the sheriff?" Even yesterday she wouldn't have had the nerve to check up on Rick like that. But this was too important.

"Search and Rescue will," Rick told her. "We don't know she's dead, there's no body, so we aren't legally responsible for calling the sheriff." She glanced at Mark, but he was staring out the window as if he had no part in this scene. As soon as Rick indicated that the meeting was over, he disappeared.

Rick walked Julie a little way down the path, going over the same questions again with her, and asking even more probing ones about Pat's attitude lately. Had she been depressed? Was she having problems?

"The only time she seemed unlike herself," Julie reflected, "was at the cookout when she said she was ill. She seemed strange."

"How strange?"

Julie had the odd feeling that she was on trial.

"Maybe scared—I don't know."

"Scared of what?"

"Rick, I don't know."

"I want you to remember every little detail."

She looked at him. "You don't think she drowned either, do you?"

"Why else would her sweater be there?"

She tried to think. "Rick, I'm going to go back there after my swimming class and go up to the tarn myself."

He reacted strongly. "You'll do no such thing. We don't want a dead counselor on our hands."

"But I could——"

He interrupted. "Julie, if you go up there, you're fired." He veered off toward the office.

Sandy was waiting for her. "Are you all right, Julie?"

"Me? Sure."

"You look like death warmed over."

Julie winced at the word 'death.' "I wish we could reach her father," she said. "It doesn't seem right."

"She isn't in the hospital, is she?" It was a statement, not a question.

Julie took a deep breath. Tears filled her eyes,

causing her friend's concerned face to swim before her. "Sandy, I have to talk to somebody. Will you swear not to repeat what I say?"

"Of course." And Sandy listened carefully as Julie told her all she knew.

Chapter 4

It was sensible, forty-year-old Meredith who told the Assembly the story Rick had put together to explain Pat's absence. She was calm and reassuring, skillful at cutting off questions and turning their attention to Boat Night, which was coming up in a few days. On Boat Night the children teamed up into small groups and decorated the canoes; prizes were given for the most imaginative. It was always a much-looked-forward-to affair, with a special dinner beforehand and the canoes, lighted by Japanese lanterns, parading past the dock and around the cove afterward.

Julie was thinking of Pat's plan to decorate her group's canoe as an Arabian dhow with lateen-rigged sails. Pat had doubled over in laughter when Julie said she thought a dhow was a Mohammedan priest. Julie had never heard of lateen sails either, but Pat finally explained that her father was a boat nut and she tried to keep up with him.

Julie's eyes filled with tears as she walked away from Assembly. She wished she hadn't snapped at Pat about wearing her new clothes. That was harmless enough, the child liking to wear pretty clothes. If I had the money for them, I'd like it myself, Julie thought, looking down at the dark red cotton fatigue sweater that she had put on that morning because it was comfortable. Her khaki shorts were faded, and near the right pocket there was a small triangular tear.

"Hey, there." It was Joe, coming up behind her, hearty and normal as ever. He came from the direction of her cabin and she wondered for a second what he had been doing down there.

She was glad to see him. He was so safe.

He grabbed her hand in his big brown paw. "Are those tears I see in those gorgeous brown eyes?" He brought his face close to hers.

Mark brushed past them. "Excuse me," he said in a chilly voice.

"Hey, where you going—to a fire?" Joe called after him.

"Busy," Mark said, and kept going.

"You take your average New Englander," Joe said, turning back to Julie, "and you got yourself a guy that can really clam up."

While, on the whole, Julie didn't like to generalize

about people, she felt reluctantly that Joe had a point. She didn't feel like talking about Mark, though. His unwillingness to stand up for her in front of Rick still stung.

"Joe, was there any trace of Pat at all?"

"Nary a trace."

He didn't seem terribly upset, but then she realized he was probably trying to cheer her up.

"I feel so bad about her," she said.

He put his hand under her chin and tilted her face up toward his. "I know, but listen, sweetheart, Search and Rescue will find her. They do a terrific job. They found a hunting pal of mine once when none of us could locate him. It was mid-October, deep snow."

She felt reassured by his manner. "You don't think she drowned?"

For a minute he seemed to be far off in his thoughts, as if he were talking to himself. "I really don't buy that. That is a kid with good sense." Then his tone changed. "Listen, girl, you've got circles under your eyes. You're worrying too much, and that's not going to do anyone any good. How about you and me sneak out after Taps and drive into Kalispell? We can hit a few bars and have some fun. Cheer you up."

"You know we can't do that." Wistfully Julie added, "But I wish we could. I'd love to get away for a few hours." *With you,* she thought. She saw herself being escorted around town by the handsome football star. *I wonder if I'm falling in love.*

61

He leaned down and kissed her, gently at first, and then with more feeling. When they finally drew apart, Julie's head was spinning. It felt so good to know that someone *cared*.

"I really like you, Julie," he murmured, still holding her. "No kidding. I'd like for us to get together. Think about it."

When he had gone, she thought about it. It was exciting. But falling in love would be serious. He was a lot older than the kids she dated in high school. She knew instinctively that Joe would mean business. *Well, why not?* She was growing up, wasn't she?

During Rest Hour she read a chapter of a James Herriot book to the kids. Shortly after she began, there were a few minutes of stifled giggles and scuffling while Billie Jean tried to keep Jennifer from taking a book away from her. It turned out to be a torrid adult romance with a racy cover showing a man and woman clutching each other ecstatically. Julie had to confiscate it, but she found it hard to keep from laughing—she could tell they felt terribly wicked.

After Rest Hour she had her intermediate swimming class. Eight-year-old April was on the dock early as usual, trying to get up her nerve to jump in. As Julie came down the path she saw two boys sneaking up behind April and she knew what they had in mind. They were planning to push her in. It had happened before.

"Harry! Mason!" she shouted, hoping to warn April.

The boys wheeled around, looking innocent. But, caught by surprise, April teetered perilously on the edge of the dock, gave a shriek, and fell in with a splash. The boys tried hard not to laugh.

"April gets a demerit for going in before the whistle," Mason said, as April slapped the water with frantic arms and finally clambered back onto the dock.

She was coughing. "You pushed me."

"Didn't touch you," Harry retorted. He was a stocky little boy whose black hair stood up straight.

"You were going to," April said, pushing her wet hair out of her eyes. "Julie, they . . ."

"Never mind," Julie said soothingly. "But if I catch anybody pushing anybody else, they'll be grounded for a week. I mean it."

Soon all the children had gathered, waiting for her whistle. For a few minutes afterward they splashed and yelled during the five-minute free swim. Then she blew the whistle again and divided them into groups. She put April in a group where the kids were practicing putting their faces under water and counting to ten. She then assigned Mason as coach to the three children who were doing best in the class. Delighted with his new authority, Mason began by having them backstroke.

Julie started another group swimming laps, practicing their breathing. Then she took on three who were still behind the others. She stood them in shoulder-deep water and had them breast-stroke with their arms. Two of the boys were surface-diving.

She enjoyed her classes. Even when she was troubled she could forget her problem for a while as she focused on her students. It was fun to start the summer teaching kids who didn't swim at all or who were afraid of the water, and then get them experienced enough to enjoy it. Sometimes there was one like Mason who qualified for the advanced class by the middle of the summer.

Toward the end of the hour, discipline broke down, and she let them splash and yell and enjoy themselves. She had a private lesson after that. She'd promised to coach one of the older campers who wanted to get some tips on racing so he could try out for his school swim team in the fall.

Later, walking back to her cabin, she began to think about Pat again. It was her impression that Pat had said her father would be back in Nairobi on the weekend. Maybe she could go to the office and check it out, if the secretary was still there. If there was any note about the date of Pat's father's return, she could tactfully suggest to Rick that he might be able to reach him tomorrow night, Friday, or at least by Saturday morning. She realized that she had absorbed Pat's conviction that her father could accomplish anything, even finding his child on a rugged mountain half a world away.

It was nearly dinner time before Julie had a chance to go to the office. Rick's boat was back but she hadn't seen him. Probably there was no news, or he would have told her.

The secretary had gone home, but the office was unlocked. There was a light in the little store next to the office, and Julie went toward it, thinking Rick might be there. If he was, it might be better to suggest to him that he do the checking. She didn't want to make him mad.

But just before she got to the door of the store, she hesitated. Rick's and Mark's voices came clearly through the open door. They sounded angry. She backed away, not wanting to be discovered as if she were eavesdropping. But she could still hear their voices.

". . . just trying to find out," Mark was saying.

Rick interrupted him. "I'm not paying you good money for nothing."

Standing behind some bushes, Julie watched as Mark stormed out of the store and strode off. He hadn't seen her. Slowly she walked back to the office, wondering about what she had overheard. What was Rick paying Mark good money for? Had she heard them right? She almost felt afraid to trust her own ears. Was there some kind of special job Mark was getting paid to do?

Disturbed, she opened the office door and went in, still deep in thought, trying to figure out what was going on. She wanted to trust Mark, but there were so many unanswered questions, so many little things she couldn't figure out.

The room was dim, but there was enough light for her to see. Julie didn't want Rick coming in to see what she was doing when he was in such an angry mood, so she left the lights off as she crossed to the big metal file cabinet in the corner.

She had to stand on tiptoe to reach Pat's file because the drawer was deep and in the very back under R's. It was thicker than most of the others. She had it half out of the drawer when she thought she heard a slight sound. She started to turn, but something struck the back of her head and she blacked out.

Chapter 5

Julie opened her eyes and quickly closed them again. The room whirled around her, and her head felt as if it were splitting. She was lying on the office couch, and Mark was taking her pulse. Rick stood behind him, looking anxious.

When he saw that she was awake, Rick said, "What happened, Julie?"

"Give her time to come to," Mark said. Very gently he brushed the hair back from a sore place behind and above her right ear. "You got a bad wallop." His eyes were kind, almost affectionate, Julie thought, but then she told herself she must be mistaken—she wasn't thinking straight because she'd blacked out.

"I'll get Marian," Rick told them and went out the door toward the nurse's bungalow.

"I don't know what happened," Julie said, looking up into Mark's blue eyes.

"That's all right. Just take it easy. You got a real crack on your head."

She closed her eyes, feeling soothed by his manner.

In a couple of minutes Rick was back with the nurse.

"I don't know," Rick was saying. "I saw the door open, so I looked in, and there was poor Julie out like a light."

Marian examined her with brisk efficiency. "Looks like a concussion. Do you remember getting dizzy before you fell?"

"It's stuffy in here," Rick said. "Anne closes the windows before she goes home."

"I don't remember feeling dizzy," Julie said. "I thought I heard a sound and I started to turn . . ."

"What kind of sound?" Mark said.

"I don't know." She felt stupid, not knowing the answers to anything. She must have fainted, but it was odd, as she had never done that before in her life. Even though it hurt, Julie turned her head away from them, facing the sofa cushion to her side. She felt confused and depressed. She was making a mess of everything!

"You must have imagined the sound," Rick said. "There was no one and nothing here when I looked in. Not even a chipmunk." He gave her a smile. To Marian he said, "Should I run her in to the hospital?"

"No," Julie said quickly as an alarm went off in her

head. "I'm all right." The idea of Rick taking her to the hospital, where Pat was supposed to be and wasn't, scared her for some reason.

"I'm quite sure it's not a fracture," Marian said. "Her pulse is a bit rapid but not too much. Maybe the hospital could take some pictures . . ."

"No," Julie said again. She looked at Mark. Even though he'd been so brusque earlier, now she felt he was her friend. He'd understand.

"I had a concussion once," Mark spoke up, coming through for her. "I know how you feel." And to Rick he said, "Let her take a day off and rest up."

Rick looked at Marian. "Mark seems to have it all settled," he observed, sarcasm in his voice.

"All she needs is to be let alone."

For a moment no one spoke; the air crackled with tension.

Then Julie smiled at Mark. "Thanks. I'll be resting in my cabin."

When Julie got up, however, she wasn't so sure. She felt shaky and dizzy and was glad that Marian insisted on walking her back to her cabin. Maybe she really had had a touch of vertigo before she passed out. It seemed strange, though, that she should have hit her head so near the back. Maybe when she had started to turn, it had thrown her off balance. She gave up thinking about it for the time being, it made her head pound.

Carol and the girls were very sympathetic. They

tucked her into bed, and Jennifer set up her little radio where Julie could reach it. Billie Jean loaned her her beloved balsam pillow and Julie didn't have the heart to tell her that, while she usually liked the smell, it was making her feel ill now. Mary gave her the latest teen romance, and Allie put her colorful afghan over Julie's feet. Carol surveyed the scene with a smile. "That's great. Now everybody out," she ordered. "Let her get some sleep."

Julie was asleep in minutes. . . .

When she woke up, Mark was standing beside her with a tray of food. She struggled to sit up. "How nice of you!"

He grinned a little self-consciously. "Even the wounded must eat."

Why is he being so nice all of a sudden? Julie wondered. *Maybe he's sorry for the way he acted. Maybe he likes me a little,* she thought, her heart beating more quickly.

Mark pulled up a camp stool and sat down. "What do you think really happened in the office?"

Had Rick sent him over to find out what she knew? Immediately, she dismissed the thought. Balancing the tray on her knees, Julie said, "I honestly don't know. I thought I heard a faint sound, but maybe I imagined it, or it might have been anything—a chipmunk outside the window—whatever. Then a sort of flash of light in my head, and that's all till I woke up on the couch."

He frowned, looking thoughtful. She wished he

would stay awhile and talk to her. Glancing at his hands, she saw they were tanned and muscular, with long fingers. She was sure they were not the hands of anyone who would hit somebody on the head. But why was she even thinking a crazy thing like that? What made her think anybody had hit her? That wouldn't make sense.

"I wonder . . ." he began. Then he stopped, hearing a commotion outside the cabin.

Singing "I Love You Truly" in a loud off-key voice, Joe marched into the cabin carrying a dinner tray. He stopped short in mock dismay. "Oh, no! Don't tell me Sir Galahad beat me to it. Come, come, you don't want that tray. This is the one with the real goodies. Look! Chocolate cake! Lamb chop specially broiled for the lamb chop with the aching head. Coffee brewed by my own adoring hands."

He put his tray on top of Julie's trunk and removed Mark's tray, putting it in Mark's lap. He put his own tray in Julie's lap. Julie giggled. She couldn't help laughing at Joe's antics. Then she saw Mark's grim face and stopped laughing. He stood up with his tray.

"Mark," she said, feeling genuinely upset, "don't go."

He gave her a look and pushed past Joe.

"Hey, fella," Joe said, "don't go off mad. Julie can eat both meals. Let's see, what have you got?" He blocked Mark's way and peered at the dishes. "Soup. Toast. Cottage cheese. Invalid fare. But our princess is

71

no invalid . . . Hey!" He looked annoyed as Mark sidestepped him and strode down the path carrying his tray. Then he whooped with laughter. "What a spoilsport! These Yankees, they can't take a joke."

"Joe, you shouldn't have done that," Julie scolded him, gently. A part of her wanted to run after Mark and thank him for his thoughtfulness, but Joe was already sitting on her bed preparing to spoon-feed her.

He stayed quite a while, telling her funny stories. He leaned toward her, suddenly serious. "I'm sorry you cracked your head. I really am. Take it easy, honey, and let me know if there's anything I can do."

Some time after he had gone, Julie got up to look for a clean pair of pajamas in her trunk. She was going to take Mark's advice and stay in bed awhile. She really did feel very woozy.

She opened her trunk drawer and gasped. It was a mess! Everything had been pulled out and jammed back in again. Her leather writing case was open, letters scattered. Who on earth had done this? And what could they possibly have been looking for? She felt outraged. She had a strong sense of privacy, and she was sure the girls understood that they were not to touch her things. Could one of them have been looking for a candy bar or something?

She went around to the other side of the cabin to see if there were any telltale candy wrappers lying around. She saw nothing out of the ordinary, until she looked at Pat's trunk. A bright scarf hung half out of the trunk. She opened the drawer. Pat's things, too, had been rifled through. Pat was very neat about her clothes, if about nothing else.

Feeling dizzy, Julie went back and sat down on her bed. What was going on? A mysterious blow on the head, her belongings ransacked . . . Then a chill went through her as she realized that whoever had gone through her trunk had deliberately left it messy. But why? Was it some sort of warning?

It made no sense. Yet that frightened her even more. Because, if something dangerous was going on, she'd better get to the bottom of it fast—before whoever was involved got to her.

Chapter 6

"It scares me," Julie said to Sandy, who was seated at the edge of her bunk bed. The cabin was empty, except for the two counselors. "Somebody searching my trunk. And Pat's too. I can't make any sense of it."

"I don't get it either." Sandy pursed her small mouth into a thoughtful O. "There are a lot of things I don't get."

"Me too. At first I thought everything was being done to find Pat, but now I'm not so sure. I understand why Rick wants to protect the camp, but recently I've begun to suspect that *nothing*'s being done."

"Wait a minute, Julie, what about the following evidence? Item one: Joe went to hunt for her. That makes sense. Joe knows the country, and we know

Moonstone

he'd be thorough. Item two: Rick called in Search and Rescue."

"He says."

Sandy raised her eyebrows. "You don't believe him?"

"Oh, I guess." Julie shrugged her shoulders. "I'd like to believe him. But Search and Rescue would be in touch with the sheriff, and you'd think the sheriff would come over here or send somebody to kind of check up on things. I mean even if Rick isn't letting the news go public, you'd think the sheriff would send somebody, kind of undercover, to talk to a few campers or counselors to find out stuff."

"Maybe he has and we don't know it."

"Sandy, we'd know if there was a stranger prowling around," Julie said, exasperated.

"And searching trunks?"

Julie made a face. "If it was the sheriff, he's a very untidy lawman."

"Yeah," Sandy agreed. "And what I particularly don't like is that crack on the head you got."

"Oh, I guess I did faint or something."

"People just don't faint," Sandy said, getting up as Jennifer and Mary tramped noisily into the cabin. "Anyway, just take it easy."

"Sandy," Jennifer said, "stay. We're giving Julie a party!" Regan and Allie followed behind her with armsful of Diet Coke, root beer, cookies, and cheese crackers, from the store.

"Thanks, but I've got to go ride herd on my own tribe."

"Don't tell 'em we're partying," Mary pleaded, half jokingly. "That Isabel of yours would knock the cabin down to get at cheese crackers."

Sandy laughed. "Mum's the word."

As the girls got busy opening their bottles and cans and packages, Julie said quietly to Sandy, "I wish I could talk to Mark."

"Oh, him," Sandy said with a dismissive wave of her hand. "The last time I saw him, Dana had him cornered in the Counselors' Room, giving him the 'oh, you're so wonderful' approach."

"Do you think he really goes for Dana?" Julie asked with a sinking heart. She'd forgotten about her co-swimming coach.

"Honey child, any man will go for the 'wonderful' bit." She waved. "I got to go do my duty. Take care."

Julie leaned back on her pillows, depressed by her doubts.

"For her majesty, the Queen," Allie announced, dumping a handful of cookies, crackers, and potato chips into Julie's lap and handing her an unopened root beer.

"Ta da!" Mary cried, spreading an opened Kleenex over Julie's chest.

Julie had meant to question them about the trunks, but their thoughtfulness about the little "party" made her decide to do it some other time. *Don't get para-*

noid, she told herself. *There's probably a perfectly reasonable explanation.* And she did her best to try and enjoy the party.

The next morning Julie woke about an hour before Reveille. She liked waking up before the girls did. It gave her a brief quiet time to herself. It was a gray morning, cool and foggy, and she lay still for a few minutes, comfortable in her warm bunk, feeling peaceful and content.

Then she glanced across at Pat's bunk, and everything came flooding back. She closed her eyes again and thought about Joe, wishing she could just go away with him somewhere for the day, just forget everything and be carefree. Joe was so much fun to be with, and he really was sweet.

Her thoughts turned to Mark, and Julie felt a different feeling stir within her. She wished she knew whether he was to be trusted or not. Sometimes he was so kind, almost as if he really liked her, but at other times he was remote and mysterious. She wondered about the snatch of conversation she had overheard between Rick and Mark. Could Rick possibly have some kind of hold on Mark? Was he paying him off in some way? They had known each other back East, after all. She remembered Sandy saying, "Why is Rick pressuring you? Why doesn't he come down hard on Mark? Mark was there too, after all. He had as much responsibility as you had, and maybe Pat is your kid, but Ham is Mark's."

Julie got up, impatient with herself. It did no good to go around and around about these things—she needed more information. She decided that she had no choice but to sneak out during Rest Hour, leaving Carol to look after the kids, while she went back to the mountain and looked around. Maybe it was futile. But this waiting around was driving her crazy! She had to do *something*.

After showering, Julie examined herself critically in the mirror. She still looked pale; her short, curly blond hair was wet and plastered to her head, and there were circles under her gold-flecked brown eyes. Eyes like placer, Joe, who'd spent last summer panning for gold in a stream near Butte, had told her. She had laughed. Placer, she'd pointed out to him, was gravel, and who wanted to be told she had gravelly eyes?

As she dressed, she saw that Pat's makeup was still scattered on the counter top: two lipsticks, eye shadow and liner, suntan lotion, cream. The sight of them gave her a sharp pang. Quickly she gathered up everything and took the cosmetics back to Pat's trunk so no one would "borrow" them.

The whole time, though, she couldn't stop thinking about how angry Rick would be if he knew she was planning to go back to the mountain. It was a risk she would have to take, however. Usually no one was prowling around during Rest Hour. In the old days, when she was a camper, they were supposed to take a nap or at least lie down and be still. It had been agony sometimes. Now the children read or were allowed to play quiet games like checkers.

Carol woke up, yawned, and turned off her alarm before it had time to go off. She always seemed to wake up right on time. Mumbling, " 'Morning," to Julie, she gathered up clothes and bath towel and went off to the showers.

Julie wondered if Rick would really fire her if he found out she had gone to look for Pat. If she was quick about it, she could easily get back in time for her swim class. Well, she thought defiantly, even if he did find out and fired her, it was more important to find Pat than to protect her job.

She felt rather pleased with herself for making that decision in spite of the risk. Being a teenager was a funny in-between period when you felt an overwhelming desire to be independent and decide things for yourself, while being obligated, at the same time, to abide by other people's rules. The bottom line seemed to be that she always had to do what other people said: her parents, her teachers, and in this case her camp director. Maybe when she got to college it would be a freer time. Anyhow, today she was making a decision on her own and she was going to stick to it. Pat had to be found.

At the last note of Reveille the girls began to wake

up, groaning and complaining. Mary was the first one out of bed. She yawned mightily and moaned, "How can any day turn out good that starts with having to get up?"

Julie laughed. Mary amused her. With her pale yellow hair, her high cheekbones, and her surprised-looking blue eyes, she reminded Julie of a doll she'd had once.

Later, after breakfast, Sandy steered Julie away from her canoeing class, who were on the beach planning and starting their Boat Night entries.

"I have to go to play rehearsal," Sandy whispered, "but I wanted to tell you I heard something odd."

"What?"

"About Ham. I heard through the grapevine that he took a canoe out yesterday without permission. He got caught and now he's grounded."

"Where was he going?"

"He'd already been. He doesn't say where, but he was coming from the direction of Bear Mountain."

"He must have been looking for Pat," Julie said excitedly.

Sandy nodded. "Looks like it. Also, somebody swiped a bunch of food from the supply room. Ham's been accused of it, but he's not talking."

"Food?" Julie thought about it. Of course. "If he thought he could find Pat, he'd know she'd be hungry . . ."

"That was my thinking too."

"How did you know all this?" Julie asked.

"My dear cabin child, Isabel, the Perfect Camper. Knows all, tells all. For the good of the cabin, of course."

"How did *she* know?"

"She's a skilled eavesdropper. She claims she 'just happened to hear' Rick cross-examining Ham."

They were interrupted by two girls who surrounded them, clamoring for attention as they begged their counselors to take a look at the sail they'd just made. Julie and Sandy turned to see a striped sail made of strips of cloth sewn together.

"Julie, do you like it? It's called Mark's Miracle."

Amused, Julie glanced at Sandy and raised her eyebrows. "Why?"

"I'm sure I'll hear it later," Sandy said with a wink. " 'Bye," and she left.

"Because," one of them explained, "Mark is always telling us about this sailboat his brother has, with weird striped sails."

"In"—the other giggled—"a place called Marblehead, Mass. Can you believe it? Marble-Head?"

"Why don't you call it the Marbleheader instead, then?" Julie said, and then thought, *Why don't I shut up and let them call the boat what they want?* She realized that she felt a touch jealous because *she* didn't know about Mark's brother and his boat at Marblehead. It seemed as if the kids had gotten to know Mark so much better than she had. "No, really, it's great," she said. "Mark's Miracle—that sounds fine. He'll like that."

"We hope so, since he's one of the judges."

"That's political bribery," she said, pretending to be shocked but unable to hide her smile.

"Huh?"

"Nothing. That's fine. But you'd better sew over those stitches between the red and the green strips. They're unraveling already."

As the kids ran off, Julie thought, *I suppose Rick will blame me because I didn't notice there was a canoe missing.* It was part of her job to check on the canoes, to see that they were all accounted for and up on their racks, paddles stashed away in the tiny boathouse. Anyone qualified to take out a canoe was supposed to sign their name on a list, specifying which canoe they had taken, where they were going, and when they would be back. Because of the knock on her head yesterday, she hadn't made her usual after-dinner checkup. She should have asked Carol or Dana or someone to do it for her. She *had* looked at the list this morning, but Ham's name, of course, wasn't on it. If only she could talk to Ham herself, but Mark would probably resent the intrusion. She had to admit that she would feel the same way if he went to her cabin and began questioning one of her girls. It just wasn't done.

As Julie surveyed the campers from her dock, she saw that some of the boys were building masts and various unidentifiable gadgets for their Boat Night creations. There was a pleasant smell of wood chips, and the sound of hammers and keyhole saws mingled with snatches of conversation. Aaron was complaining that he needed a real saw, not the tiny keyhole. Julie sympathized, but it was against the rules. Regulation-sized saws could be dangerous, she explained.

"Dangerous!" he scoffed. "Me and my dad use real tools all the time. Where's Ham, anyway? He's supposed to help me."

"He's under house arrest," piped up the all-knowing Isabel.

"Oh, yeah?" Aaron said, but he was already drifting away, back to the strange square frame he was making that he and his group hoped was going to make this canoe look like an old-time schooner. He had torn a picture out of a magazine and was using that for a pattern.

Julie was surprised and interested to see these land-locked kids becoming fascinated by oceangoing crafts. She had expected most of them to come up with versions of the boats on Flathead Lake and Whitefish Lake that she herself was familiar with. But they were more creative and imaginative than that.

She sat down on the sand and answered questions about measurements and angles as best as she could.

She was feeling a little dizzy again and her head ached. It seemed to come and go.

Joe came over, dressed in his riding boots and smelling slightly horsey, and sat down beside her. "What a cushy job you've got," he said. "I've just spent an hour in the hot sun trying to teach two kids how not to fall off a horse. I mean the summer's half over and they're still falling off." He mopped his forehead. "I think I'd rather be in football training."

Julie laughed, then her expression grew serious.

"Joe, what's the story about Ham?"

"Ham?" He looked blank for a moment. "Oh yeah, Ham. I heard he took off in a canoe yesterday by himself. Stole some food, too. That kid's all mixed up."

"When you were looking for Pat, was there any clue at all?"

"Not a thing." He stretched out on his back in the sand. "I'm afraid she's gone, sweetie. I'm sorry, but I'm afraid she is."

He sounded so calm it bothered her. "Doesn't that upset you?"

His eyes were closed. "That kid's disappearance is the best thing that ever happened to me."

"What! What do you mean?" She was horrified.

He opened his eyes and sat up. "Mean? I didn't mean that—I don't even know what I said, let alone what I meant. I think I have sunstroke. Those dumb

85

kids, they won't learn to hug the horse with their knees. You'd think they were some kind of Eastern dudes, they're so stupid about horses."

She studied him. "You just like to sound tough. Inside you're a big marshmallow."

He laughed. "You found me out." He kissed her lightly and got to his feet. "I gotta go. I'm going to get a cold drink, then I'm taking a bunch of kids around the lake. Cross your fingers that they don't fall off."

"I'll walk you as far as the Hash House." She blew her whistle. "Break time. Milk at the Hash House."

The kids dropped their tools and raced up the path, all except Aaron, who lingered another minute to finish driving in a nail. Then he, too, raced past them, yelling, "Here comes the Milk Express! Make way for the Milky Way!"

As they walked, Julie wondered if she should tell Joe about her trunk. It disturbed her to think that somebody had searched her things, as if they thought she might be guilty—but of what? Of trying to cover up her own negligence? She shook her head, frowning.

At the place where the path branched off in one direction to the Hash House and in the other to the stable, Joe stopped and kissed her again, warmly this time. He felt reassuring and comfortable and at the same time exciting. He lifted her off her feet and kissed her again, more demandingly.

Someone behind them coughed a phony "excuse me" cough. Embarrassed, Julie glanced back. Jennifer and Mary were on the path, doubled up with laughter.

Coolly Joe said, "Don't you young ladies know enough to knock?"

This remark sent them into new convulsions of giggles.

"It's our space as much as yours, Joe," Mary said.

Joe looked around. "Why, so it is. I swear, I did think I was in the hospital cabin. I like to keep the patients cheered up, and this young lady has a busted head."

"You're the one to cheer 'em up, Joe," Jennifer said.

"Why, thank you. I appreciate that." To Julie he said, "Take two and call me in the morning."

The girls were still giggling after he had gone. "Joe is too much," Jennifer said. "So, Julie, how do you feel—any better?"

The question sent Mary into new peals of laughter.

Julie was annoyed to find herself blushing. Joe might think it was all a joke, but she felt as if her authority was undermined when her campers could laugh at her.

Suddenly Mary stopped laughing and said in a small voice, "Julie, when is Pat coming back?"

For a moment Julie was startled. She had forgotten that the girls still thought Pat was in the hospital. She felt a lump in her throat and she tried to swallow. "Soon, I hope. Listen, I have to go—my kids are probably throwing milk at each other by now."

"Julie?" Jennifer's voice stopped her.

"What?"

"Don't mind us. I mean we know how Joe is."

She didn't know what to say, so she waved and kept walking. *We know how Joe is*. What did they know? she wondered. What did they think he was like? Maybe she saw him differently from the way others did. Feeling hopelessly confused, Julie trudged on. When she rounded the bend and saw what lay ahead, her eyes widened.

"Mason!" she yelled. "No!"

And Mason checked his throwing arm in mid-air and drank the milk as if he had no intention of throwing it at his cabin mate.

Chapter 7

Carol was playing Scrabble with Jennifer, Allie, and Billie Jean, and the others were reading, when Julie left the cabin at the start of Rest Hour. No one had questioned her about where she was going. She knew they assumed she would spend the period in the Counselors' Room.

She walked quickly along the path to the beach, glad that she didn't encounter anyone except a couple of girls who were running from the infirmary, where they'd gotten poison ivy medicine, to get to their cabin before their counselors gave them a demerit for being late.

There was no one at all in the vicinity of the beach. She signed herself out and took one of the fiberglass canoes. It would have been fun to use Rick's motorboat but he had locked it up; besides, everybody would hear the motor. And, she added silently to herself, I have no right at all, under any circumstances, to make off with Rick's boat.

There was still a light mist on the lake, which was just as well in case anyone was looking. She felt sneaky, even though she wasn't really doing anything wrong, she reminded herself, and tried to hug the shore, hoping to keep out of sight. But nothing really mattered as much as finding Pat. If the child was still alive. Julie thought about Joe's strange remarks and told herself it was because he didn't like to show emotion. He even made a joke of love. She wondered what would happen if a person were to take him seriously.

She paddled with a long, steady stroke, giving just the right twist to her paddle at the end of the stroke to keep the canoe on course. Canoeing was something she had learned when she was young, and she'd always loved it. The dip of the paddle, the long push against the force of the water, the shooting forward . . . When she was little she used to pretend she was an Indian guide leading Lewis and Clark through the waters of northwestern Montana.

There were a couple of outboards cruising slowly along the far side of the lake, heading in the direction of the little settlement of Vinegar Cove. She kept close to the shore line, not only to avoid being seen, but because there was a strong breeze coming up, which was blowing the fog away and stirring up the lake. She knew from experience that the water could get really rough.

The tallest mountains some distance away were sprinkled with new snow. This was on top of the hardened crust that never melted. In another six weeks or so there would be even more snow and the trees would start to turn. She loved hiking up a mountain in the fall, when the western larch had turned color and you could walk in a shower of golden needles. She was glad she would be at the university, with the majestic Mount Sentinel nearby.

She thought about Pat. Was it possible that Pat had hidden out somewhere as some kind of crazy joke? But that would be cruel, and Pat might be ornery but she wasn't cruel. Julie thought about Ham and the food. His stealing food didn't seem to make sense unless he knew where she was and was taking the food to her. On the other hand, maybe Pat had really gone off to "go to the bathroom," as he'd delicately put it, and maybe she had gotten lost, and Ham had simply hoped to find her yesterday. But wouldn't he have explained all that? Well, all right, he *did* explain it. That was exactly what he'd said, but he was behaving so strangely it was hard to believe Ham didn't know something more.

As she got closer to the beach, she tensed up. If she turned her head quickly, she felt dizzy again. Better be careful. She began to feel nervous. How could she expect to find anything when Search and Rescue and Joe and Rick and that Al person hadn't? Maybe it was foolish even to try.

But Julie didn't turn back. When she got to the beach she found it hard to believe that a throng of happy kids had been having fun here so short a time ago. Now the beach looked cold and unfriendly; nothing remained of the cookout except the charred wood of the campfire. For the first time she began to feel that Pat really had drowned.

The climb was not long but it was steep, and Julie had to stop often to get her breath. The air in the woods seemed cold and oppressive. Her head began to throb. She knew Ham was right about the cave; it was around here somewhere. When she was a camper she'd heard rumors about it, but the woman who was camp director then told them not to look for it because they might run into a wild animal who was using it for shelter. As a result, Julie had no idea where it was.

She stopped to rest after a little while, confident that she was close to the tarn. The trees had thinned out and there were big boulders here and there, moss-covered and ancient-looking. She noticed an underground stream had seeped through to the surface, making the path wet in places. As she leaned against a rock to rest, a white-tailed deer broke from cover, gave her a startled look, and crashed off through the woods.

Julie started up again. She wanted to get this over with and get back.

For some reason the deer made her think of Mark. Why? She searched her mind for the connection. Long-legged? Long eyelashes? Elusive? She smiled at the thought. Bambi.

Suddenly the tarn was in front of her. It was nearly hidden by the tall, jagged rocks. As she had remembered, it was beautiful in a scary sort of way. The water was blue-black, shadowed by the overhanging rocks. In the middle a shred of cloud was reflected, moving swiftly, then gone. The air was cold.

A thought had been haunting her. If Pat had drowned, her body would have surfaced by now—unless it was caught somehow under a rocky ledge or tangled in whatever grew at the bottom of the lake. Anyone who fell into such icy water would be paralyzed in a minute or two. And even if the water were not so cold, climbing out would be difficult if not impossible, since a person would have to scramble up sheer rock faces.

Her heart beating fast, Julie headed for one of the smaller rock formations, where she would get a good view of the tarn. She climbed up, cutting the palm of her hand on a jagged surface.

When she reached the uneven top, she clung to it and peered down. The water was so calm it looked like solid rock, and she had the feeling that if she fell, she would bounce off the surface. There was no body to be seen anywhere. From her height, the tarn looked like a small oval in hollowed earth, the rocks an irregular iron setting for a deadly black jewel.

It was deathly still. No birds twittered in the woods, no insects rippled the surface of the lake. Behind her the trees loomed up like threatening arms ready to grab her. Julie remembered that under the best of circumstances she didn't like heights. As she peered down into the mesmerizing blackness, she suddenly felt dizzy. Her body was off balance and there was a sickening lurch forward. Quickly, Julie threw herself backward in reaction, grabbing wildly for a more secure hold on the rock. But the edge crumpled as she seized it and she cried out. She was slipping . . .

Hands grabbed her hard by the arm and pulled her sharply around and up until she was on the firm surface of rock again.

It was Mark and he was furious. "Don't you think we have trouble enough without you killing yourself?" he said angrily. "What exactly do you think you were doing?"

She was trembling all over. "I was looking for Pat."

"Oh, and you were going to do that by jumping into a bottomless lake and paddling around in the nice ink-black water for a while?"

94

Now she was mad at herself, partly due to her release from fear, partly because she resented his anger. "For that matter, what are *you* doing here, sneaking up on people?" she retorted.

"Saving you from instant death, for one thing," Mark practically shouted. "I was just in time."

"Did you know I was here?"

He hesitated. "I saw you leave."

"And you wanted to check up on me. Who sent you after me?"

Flushing with anger, Mark replied, "I'm nobody's errand boy."

"Then why did you follow me?" Julie persisted. "You stayed out of sight, too, so I wouldn't see you. Why did you want to know where I was going?" In spite of what he said, she thought Rick must have sent him.

Mark's mouth was tight and there were white lines around it. "I could care less what you're doing. I want to find that kid."

She made a gesture toward the lake and her voice was tight with tears. "Good luck." She slid down off the rock and headed for the trail.

"Julie?"

She heard him call but she ignored him. She was upset that he had followed her, as if he suspected her of something—or as if he'd wanted to know if she knew something. It irked her that she had gotten into a dangerous situation and had had to be rescued by him.

95

Why hadn't he stayed back in old Marble-Head on his stupid boat with the gaudy sail?

The wind was at her back going up the lake, and she made good time. She was anxious to get back to camp before Rick found out she had gone. It would be stupid to get fired over such a futile trip.

Joe was in the cove watering one of his horses. "How's the lady of the lake?" he called, as she brought the canoe in.

At least *he* didn't get mad and yell at her all the time.

"Fine, Joe, how are you?" She made herself smile.

He looped the reins over his arm and held the canoe steady while she got out. The horse snorted, throwing up a spray of water. "Where you been?"

"Trying to figure out what happened to Pat."

He did a double take. "You mean you went back there?"

"Yes."

He frowned. "Not smart, honey, not smart. You want to get yourself fired? Old Rick the Ranger, he don't like outside help." He looked grim for a minute. "Or likes it too much, one or the other."

She didn't know what he meant, but she wasn't ready for another lecture. She changed the subject, and soon Joe was smiling again as they walked along the path away from the beach, the big roan stomping heavily behind them.

As they parted, Joe said, "Take my advice, sweetie,

don't run around playing detective. You'll get yourself in trouble." Julie nodded. She was tired and wished she could lie down for a few minutes, but she had just enough time before class to wash up and change into her swimsuit.

Later, during dinner, Julie felt Rick's eyes on her. She stirred uneasily, tried to reassure herself that so far he had not mentioned her absence. Ham was in his place, but he looked pale and he was not talking.

"Julie," Mary said, "if you're not going to eat your french fries . . ."

Julie slid her plate toward Mary. "Help yourself."

"Pig!" Allie said under her breath to Mary.

"Nope, just a quick thinker," Mary replied brightly.

"I heard we're having butterscotch pudding for dessert," Billie Jean said.

There was a united groan.

"Not again!" Jennifer complained.

Allie said quickly, "I'll swap my salad for anybody's pudding."

"You mean you *like* butterscotch pudding?" Billie Jean was already sliding Allie her plate. Within minutes she had promises of four more puddings. "Enough already!" she said. "How many puddings do you think I can eat?"

"That's an interesting question," Mary answered. "Anybody want to place a bet?"

Julie was feeling cheered up by their nonsense until the counselor at the next table leaned over and asked her what news there was of Pat. Immediately, all the conversation turned to Pat. Mary made the situation even worse by saying she wanted to send flowers to Regional Hospital, where Meredith had said Pat was going.

Julie looked over and saw that Rick was listening to the sudden buzz of questions and speculations about Pat. Finally he stood up and rapped his knife against his water glass for attention. "I want you to know," he announced with his all-enveloping smile, "that Pat is doing fine. Her dad is going to take her home as soon as he gets back to this country. Later you can all write to her."

"I want to make her a ceramic ashtray," Jennifer said, and everyone laughed. "That's what I'm working on in ceramics," she added defensively.

"I don't think Pat has taken up smoking," Rick said. "But thank you all for your concern." He sat down again.

Julie shuddered. It was ghoulish, talking like that. And he had sounded so convincing that for a moment she'd believed he really had found Pat and taken her to the hospital. She glanced at Ham and saw the tight look of horror on his face. He shoved back his chair and ran from the room.

"What's with him?" Allie asked.

Julie groped for an answer. "Umm, he hasn't been feeling well," she said.

"He must have heard about the butterscotch pudding," Mary joked.

One thing Julie was sure of—she was going to have to talk with Ham.

Chapter 8

After dinner that night, while the girls in her cabin were stitching and patching together decorations for their boat, Julie thought about Ham. She would probably have to go to Mark's cabin to find him, and that would make Mark mad all over again. Everybody was beginning to see her as an interfering nuisance. *Tough luck, Mark,* Julie thought. *You're not going to boss me around anymore. I'm doing what I think is right.*

"I've got this almost done." Mary held up a crazy patchwork of sail.

"What is it?" Allie asked.

"Name it and you can have it," Jennifer said, and ducked the pillow Mary threw at her.

"It's for a UFO boat," Mary said. "From outer space."

Billie Jean laughed. "What a super idea. That way, you can goof up all you want and call it extraterrestrial."

"It should have a robot sailor," Jennifer said.

Regan examined it, thoughtful in her scholarly looking glasses. "I don't think the colors out in space are the same as ours. For instance, some planets have yellow skies."

"Oh, Regan, don't be so intellectual," Allie said.

Regan laughed and blushed. "I read it somewhere."

Julie left them arguing about what colors Mary's sail would be in other atmospheres. She knew if she were going to go find Ham, she would have to do it now, before she lost her nerve.

She walked quickly in the direction of the boys' cabins. Luckily Mark's was the nearest, so she wouldn't have to parade past a whole group of boys' cabins. They didn't like having women prowling around, as Rick had put it with his smile. Sometimes a few boys would stray into the girls' area, and more than once girls had been thrown out of the boys' area, but on the whole everyone respected the privacy rule. She thought of her mother telling Aunt Harriet, "Julie has a good sense of propriety. I don't have to worry about her doing outrageous things." *Well, Mom, your one and only dutiful daughter is breaking rules right and left.*

She didn't see anyone in or around Mark's cabin, but as she got close she heard voices. Then she saw

Mark and Ham sitting on the steps of the cabin, their backs toward her. Julie paused; her stomach was in knots and she was tempted to simply turn and flee. But she forced herself to stay.

Ham was in tears, and Mark had his arm around the boy's shoulders.

"If you'd just tell me all about it, Ham," Mark was saying. "You know you can trust me." His voice was so gentle, Julie hardly recognized it.

"I promised," Ham sobbed. "I can't tell. I promised."

Mark brushed the boy's hair back from his forehead. "Circumstances alter cases sometimes. Situations change, and even promises have to be broken. Not usually, but in an emergency . . ."

Julie realized she was eavesdropping. She had to get out of there. She turned quietly, but a branch under her foot gave a loud crack. Ham and Mark turned quickly and saw her. Ham looked horrified.

"I'm sorry," Julie stammered. "I just wanted to ask Ham if I could help . . ."

Ham jumped up and ran into the cabin, slamming the screen door. Mark stood up. Julie couldn't read his face, but he didn't look angry.

"I'm sorry," she said again. "I didn't mean to . . ."

Mark shook his head. "Let's talk." He started along a side path that swept around behind the boys' cabins and into the woods.

She followed him, having to hurry to keep up with

his long stride. She wondered briefly if he was going to bawl her out again. When Mark came to a clearing where a wide seat was nailed between two trees, he sat down. He held out his hand, and she sat down beside him.

He was quiet for a moment, keeping her hand in his as if he had forgotten it was there. "I'm sorry I was so nasty up at the tarn," he said finally. "You scared me when you almost fell into that hell-hole."

Julie swallowed, all kinds of thoughts and emotions flickering through her mind. Just when she was prepared for another battle, Mark surprised her again. "Well," she began, "I was nasty too. Thank you for saving me." She studied his profile out of the corner of her eye. Greek, she thought; he looks like one of those Greek coins. Or was it Roman? He had classic features, anyway. But the face on a coin was hard and cold, and Mark's face at the moment was neither.

"I can't make sense of it," he said.

"Me either." She felt a rush of relief that he was going to talk to her about it.

He looked at her. "Do you know Joe very well?"

"Joe?" That was the last thing she had expected Mark to say.

"Yeah. I know he hangs around you, but do you know much about him?"

"Well, everybody who reads the Montana papers knows quite a lot about him, especially during football season."

"So what do you know, besides how good he is at tackling?"

She tried to remember. "He comes from a little town east of the mountains, called Two Dot."

Mark made a face, and she remembered what Al had said about Montana place names.

"His dad is a ranch hand. He's got a lot of brothers and sisters. He's in college on a four-year football scholarship. Why?"

"Poor family?"

"I suppose so. Ranch hands aren't millionaires."

"Know anything about his private life? I mean can you think of anything he might be blackmailed for?"

She stared at him. How had Mark gotten that idea? "Blackmailed! What do you mean?"

He shook his head. "I don't know what I mean. I overheard a snatch of conversation. Not enough to get it, but it sounded as if Rick had something on Joe." He gave himself a little shake. "I probably read it wrong. I don't have any great love for either of those guys. Maybe subconsciously I want to hear rotten things about them."

"Why did you come here if you don't like it?" Julie asked, fascinated.

"I hadn't seen this part of the country before, thought it'd be a good experience. Even more importantly, the money is good. I need it for college." He laughed. "Maybe that's kind of blackmail, too." He stood up, letting go of her hand. For a moment he looked down at her, then he leaned over and kissed her on the mouth.

Before she could recover from her astonishment, Mark was gone. She put her hand to her face. It hadn't been like Joe's fervent kisses. It was almost tender, firm but gentle. What about Dana, though—wasn't Mark involved with her? She wanted to call him back, but other thoughts stopped her. She had thought he disliked her, but do you kiss someone you don't like? Feeling strangely happy, Julie jumped up from her wooden seat. She was halfway back to her cabin before an awful thought struck her. Maybe Mark was playing up to her, trying to get something on Joe. To put himself in the clear, perhaps. Suddenly the idea of Joe being blackmailed seemed ridiculous.

Julie wanted to believe that Mark was her friend. She longed to confide in him, to tell him about her trunk being searched—that preyed on her mind. But she had to be careful.

As she continued back to the cabin, she kept looking over her shoulder. It was dark. She had the uneasy feeling that she was being followed, but when she glanced back, no one was there. *Don't get paranoid,* she told herself. Obviously, all this mystery was getting to her.

When she came to the office she slowed down. What if she got Pat's father's address in Africa and called him herself? It was wrong for him not to know. She could make an excuse in the morning about going over to Vinegar Cove, so her phone call wouldn't be overheard. She could say her head still ached and fake a visit to the doctor. She'd like to call home, too, and talk to her dad. He was good at unraveling mysteries.

The lights in the office were out. With trembling fingers, she unsnapped the small flashlight she carried on her belt. Rick would be furious if he found her in the files again. She mustn't let that happen. Silently, Julie entered the office, tiptoed across the room and, focusing her light on the file drawer, pulled it open. She flipped through the letters to the R's.

Reilly, Riskin, Robinson . . . She kept on through Rolfe, Rumford, Rundell, and there was the S file. She went back and flipped the R's again, more slowly. Pat Robbins's file was missing.

The overhead light went on with such a dazzling shock she let out a cry. She whirled around. Rick was standing there. It seemed like a century before he spoke. "What are you doing, Julie?" His voice was like iron.

"I was looking for Pat's file." Her voice shook. The expression in his eyes scared her.

"Why?" He took a couple of steps toward her. He was holding his arms out from his sides, his hands half-clenched. She was sure he was going to attack her.

She tried to speak calmly. "I was worried. Pat is one of my kids, after all. I was responsible for her on that trip. I . . . I was thinking about calling her father." She knew she'd been foolish to say that when she saw the fierce gleam in his eyes.

"My files are private. I don't need you snooping around. Any calling to Pat's father that is done will be done by me."

This makes twice, Julie. "Have you called him?" she blurted, almost involuntarily. It terrified her to hear herself challenging him. *What am I doing?* she thought.

Rick didn't answer. Instead he moved toward her slowly, and his silence was more frightening than anything he could have said. She stepped backward, her shoulders pressed against the file cabinet. It felt cold and hard, and the handle of the top drawer dug into her back.

"You know something that I don't know. You'd better tell me, Julie, or you'll be in trouble. Obstructing justice is a serious crime."

She gave a little gasp. He was so close to her now she could smell his after-shave. "I don't know anything. I'm trying to find out." He made a gesture toward her with his hands, and she was sure he was going to kill her.

Suddenly the door was shoved open. Joe's voice said, "Rick, I've been looking for you. About the kid, I . . ." He saw Julie and stopped short.

Rick jerked, turning around toward him. "Yes? What is it?" He moved away from Julie.

Joe looked from Rick to Julie and back again. "What's going on?"

"Going on? I don't know what you mean. Julie and I were having a little talk. A private talk," he said.

"Sorry about that," Joe said gruffly.

"What did you have to tell me?"

"Oh yeah." Joe hesitated. "Susan Mitsopulous fell off her horse. She . . . uh . . . hurt her back. Maybe you should take a look."

"Right." Rick elbowed past Joe and went out.

Joe studied Julie's face. He looked unhappy. "What was that all about?"

Julie took a deep, shaky breath. "I was trying to find Pat's file. I wanted to call her father."

Joe frowned. "Julie," he said, coming over and putting his arm around her. "Honey, stay out of it." His face softened, and for a moment he looked genuinely worried. Then his manner changed, back to the hearty Joe she knew. "Look, let's get in that rendezvous on the ball field. This is a good time for it, hey?" With his arm still around her, he steered her out of the office and down the road toward the baseball field. Julie checked her watch. It was lights-out time for the campers, but she knew that Carol would see that the kids got to bed.

She was glad of Joe's strong arm. She was still shaking. "He scared me," she said. "I thought he was going to . . . to beat me up or kill me or something."

109

"Now why would he do that? Hey, let's forget old Rick and talk about us."

They walked around the curve in the road, past the turnoff to the boys' cabins, past a stand of birches and willows, to a cleared field where the baseball diamond was. They sat down on the players' bench, looking up at the stars. It was a clear night. Joe turned her face toward him, looking at her intently for a moment, and then kissed her, a long, probing kiss.

She let herself go, into the safety of Joe's presence, his feeling for her. She kissed him back, and his arms tightened around her. The scene with Rick began to fade. He had been angry, no doubt about that, but maybe he had a right to be. She had probably imagined the menace in his eyes. It was silly to think he had meant to harm her.

"Joe," she said, pulling back a bit to look at him. "Somebody ransacked my trunk. And Pat's."

"Somebody what?"

"Went through my trunk."

He shook his head, laughing and kissing her again. "Baby, you read too many mysteries. Why would anybody want to search your trunk?"

She couldn't answer because he was kissing her.

When she tried to speak a minute later, he stopped her. "We're here, Julie, you and me. That's what it's all about." His fingers traced her lips, then his strong hands went around her again, pulling her to him tightly.

110

A little warning bell went off in her head. She wasn't ready for this. Joe was exciting and attractive and she liked him a lot, but he was kind of overpowering.

He sensed her reluctance. "What's the matter?"

"I just . . . Maybe we'd better go back now."

"After all the time I've waited to get you out here? No way." He laughed, but he sounded impatient.

"Please, Joe . . ." She backed away.

"You mean. . . ?" He looked as if he couldn't believe it.

"Yes, I like you a lot, Joe, but . . ."

He gave her a long, hard stare. Then, mimicking her voice, he said, "I like you a lot Joe, but . . . But I'm just a kid. Get a date with the football star, but don't give anything back." In his own voice he said, "I should have known."

He got up and, stuffing his hands in his pockets, he walked away.

She stood where he had left her. Tears filled her eyes. She'd thought he really cared about her, but he didn't. She was just another girl. She needed his friendship, but that wasn't what he was offering. Maybe she *was* just a stupid kid.

She started running down the road in the other direction. All she wanted to do was get into bed and turn out the light and forget everything about this stupid day. Be invisible.

Julie came fast around the bend in the road and

crashed into someone. He let out a startled "Oof!" It was Mark. "What's the matter?"

"Nothing," she said and burst into tears.

For a moment he didn't move. Then he pulled her against his shoulder. "Take it easy. Nothing's all that bad." His voice was gentle.

She leaned gratefully against him, and then in her head she heard all the doubts she had had about him. How could she trust any of these people? She pulled away and said, "I've got to get back to the cabin."

"I'll walk you there." For a few minutes he walked beside her in silence. She was glad he wasn't pressing her to find out what was wrong.

"Ham had a bad nightmare a few minutes ago," he told her. "He hasn't been sleeping well. He fell asleep and began to scream."

"What about?"

"Something about bears. He kept saying, 'The grizzly got her.' I woke him and told him there weren't any bears around here, and he said, 'I can smell 'em.' "

"There are bears in the mountains."

"Well, with all the coming and going there's been on Bear Mountain lately, there's not likely to be any there now." He seemed suddenly defensive. "I may be an Eastern dude, as your friend Joe likes to say, but I'm not totally ignorant." Mark was carrying a small branch that he had broken off as they went down the path. He slashed at a tree. "Or maybe it's crawling with bears. What do I know?"

It occurred to her that his prickliness might come from being teased about being an Easterner. *We do tend to make fun of Easterners,* she thought. Out loud she said, "You're right; a bear won't hang around if he knows people are there."

"Thanks," he said softly.

They had come to the path that led to the girls' cabins. He stopped, looking down at her. She couldn't read his expression, but she knew it was not unkind. *Oh, be my friend,* she longed to say, *I need a friend.*

Almost as if he had heard her, Mark put his hand under her chin and turned her face up to his. He leaned forward, and she knew he was going to kiss her.

But at that moment Marge and Nancy, two other counselors, came along, laughing and talking. "Uh, oh. Excuse us," Nancy said.

Mark pulled back, straightening up quickly. "Good night," he said and walked away.

Only then did Julie realize that she hadn't asked him where he'd been going before. He'd been headed in the opposite direction from her cabin. Was he going back, now, to check on something, to meet with someone?

She was glad to see that everyone in the cabin was asleep when she walked in. All she wanted to do was to bury her face in the pillow. She minded losing Joe's friendship more than she could express. He had seemed so solid, so reliable. Now he didn't like her anymore, and she felt confused enough to wonder if it wasn't really her fault. Even worse, now Rick hated her and distrusted her. And she no longer trusted Rick. No matter how she tried to rationalize the scene in the office, her instincts cried out *danger*.

Chapter 9

Julie lay awake a long time, trying to make sense out of all that had happened. Bruised by Joe's reaction, she had mixed feelings about Mark. What was she to make of Mark? One minute she trusted him, the next minute she didn't. How could he be as nice as he had been just now if he was up to something? Was anybody really what they seemed?

She wished desperately she could talk to her dad. He was good at sorting things out and making sense of them. She thought of Mark's theory that Rick was blackmailing Joe. But if he was, how did that relate to her, or to Pat's disappearance? She had the nagging feeling that there was one key fact that would make everything fall into place, but what it was, she didn't know.

At last Julie fell asleep, thinking that maybe the smartest thing to do was just not to fall in love with anybody.

She woke up a little after one o'clock and couldn't get back to sleep. After tossing and turning for a while, she decided to take a walk. The moon was full and it was a beautiful night. She put her small flashlight in her bathrobe pocket.

Walking along the path toward the tennis courts, she felt a little calmer. The woods were still except for occasional rustles and tiny squeaks. She thought about all the life that went on in the forest, day and night; there were so many things that humans never saw.

A chipmunk, startled by her approach, scampered up a yellow pine, chittering at her.

"What are you up to?" she said softly. "It's late for you to be awake."

She strolled past the courts and along the path that eventually wound around by Rick's cabin. It was darker here, where the trees were thicker, and now and then she beamed her light at the ground to make sure she didn't trip over something. When she came to the little-used path that she remembered from bird walks in her camper days, she decided to turn back. If she were found prowling around so late, it would be one more black mark against her, and she didn't need that. Turning around, Julie paused to look at the stars, very bright in a clear sky. They seemed to be hanging just above the treetops.

116

The sound of voices brought her up short. Quickly, Julie stepped off the path and ducked into the shadow of some tall pines. Prickly juniper scratched her ankles. As the sounds came closer, she heard Rick's rather high voice and a deeper rumbly one that sounded like Al's.

If she moved, she realized with growing fear, they would hear or see her. Common sense told her to just step out on the path and announce her presence. She could say she was trying to walk herself into sleepiness, which was the truth. Yet Julie remained where she was, following some other deeper instinct that told her to lie low.

She crouched down; the men were closer now. She almost stopped breathing in an effort not to be discovered. The men were arguing. She caught an occasional word, Rick saying, ". . . plans . . ." Al's voice saying, ". . . no goods, no sale . . ." It sounded like a business argument.

Then Al's voice came clearly. "You, the big judge of character. You never should have rung him in."

"That's beside the point now," Rick said.

Somewhere behind Julie an owl hooted.

"Hold it," Rick said. He played his flashlight over the path and in the direction of the woods.

Julie sank down further, ignoring the sharp juniper. The light just missed her head as she crouched close to the ground.

"Thought I heard something," Rick said.

117

"It was a stupid owl. Even I know an owl when I hear one."

"We're going to have to make other plans," Rick said.

"You're telling me! And this time leave heroes out of it."

A sudden cramp in Julie's leg made her lose her balance. She thrust out her hand to keep from falling over, and the little flashlight struck against a rock with a loud clink.

"Hey! I did hear something!" Rick had been moving away, but now Julie knew from his voice that he had turned back in her direction.

Keeping down close to the ground, she began to move quickly away, going deeper into the woods.

"Who's there?" Rick called out, his light making sweeping arcs.

Her sneakers found the bird walk trail looped in a wide half-circle through the pine and birch trees. Julie knew that eventually it led back to the cabins. She wavered. Should she run for it, or should she remain where she was? What would Rick do to her if he found her there, anyway? Julie remembered the expression on the camp director's face when he had caught her searching in the files, and abruptly she stood up and ran.

She didn't know what Rick and Al had been talking about, but deep in her bones she did know that they would not appreciate her having overheard them.

As she ducked under branches and scraped past overgrown bushes, Julie tried to keep her ears open— she could still hear them crashing through the trees. Thank goodness Rick was not much of a nature man himself, or he would be familiar with that path.

Unfortunately, she wasn't too familiar with it herself. She hadn't been on it since she was a camper. It seemed to wander on and on, and Julie began to wonder if she was mistaken in thinking it led back to the cabins. What if it came to a dead end? The trees and brush in here were too thick to get through without a path.

She paused for a breath, then heard the men, still pursuing her. *Darn!* If she only had her flashlight she could go faster, but she had dropped it. Julie started up again, trying to feel her way through the darkness. A branch slashed her across the face, and a moment later she crashed into a fir tree with a thud that she was sure they could hear. Her breath was coming in short gasps now. Her chest felt tight, and her heart was pounding, from both fear and exhaustion.

Abruptly the path curved, and she realized she must be coming around to the main path. She ran faster. If she could only get back to her cabin and into bed, she could pretend to be asleep. She stumbled again; her legs were trembling badly. *Please, please,* she prayed, *let me get back to the cabin*.

When the main path came into view at last, Julie

glanced over her shoulder and slowed down a little, not wanting to wake anybody, but still driven by the need to get out of sight. Finally she saw her own cabin. Tiptoeing in, she climbed into her bunk, pulling the blanket up around her face.

A couple of minutes later she heard quiet footsteps. Two people's steps, she was quite sure. She kept her eyes tightly shut, not daring to look. They moved slowly; they stopped in front of the cabin.

Did they suspect someone in the cabin or were they checking all of them to see if anyone was missing?

When the steps were finally out of hearing, relief flooded through her. She let her breath out in a long, quivering gasp. That had been too close for comfort!

Julie lay there for a while, trying to make sense of what she had overheard. Who was the hero they'd been talking about? Mark? Joe? Or were they talking about camp at all? It was like trying to put together a jigsaw puzzle in the dark.

Try as she might to make out the pieces, she didn't have enough light to work with. But the problem was, time was running out—definitely for Pat, if she were still alive—and after tonight, maybe for herself as well.

Chapter 10

After Assembly the next morning, the campers remained for a special treat: Sandy's play. When she announced that her drama class was putting on "a live performance of that quaint little folk play, *Six Who Pass While Lentils Boil*, the children hooted with laughter just at the title. What would they do with the play itself? Julie wondered. She glanced at Molly Hansen's parents, who had come for what Molly was calling the premiere. They looked proud and expectant.

Julie noticed Rick talking to Ham, his hand on the boy's shoulder as if they were buddies. Ham looked uncomfortable. He caught Julie's eye for a moment, and it seemed to her there was a plea for help in his expression. Maybe she was exaggerating it; lately she saw significance in everything.

Joe sat two rows in front of her. He had not spoken, and she knew she was not exaggerating *that*. Mark, on the other hand, gave her a quick, warm smile. She wondered if men were always so hard to figure out. It seemed to her that the guys she had known in high school were downright transparent compared to these two. Maybe growing up was more complicated than she had expected.

Dana sat beside her. "How's your busted skull?"

"Fine now."

"How's young April coming with putting her head under water?"

"Pretty good. She seems to be getting over her fear."

Dana nodded. Then almost to herself, she said, "There seems to be a lot of fear floating around lately." Julie looked at her, wondering what she meant, but Dana offered no explanation, and the play was starting.

The play was so dated and cutesy-quaint, it was hard to believe anyone had ever taken it seriously. Sandy had wisely played it for laughs, playing against the drippy sentimentality. Molly Hansen, in her peasant dress, with her colorless hair hanging in limp curls, was so bad she was good. The audience was in continuous laughter, except for the Hansens, who looked bewildered.

Julie's mind wasn't really on the play. All morning she thought about getting away to make that phone call in Vinegar Cove. She'd call her father first to see what he suggested. Maybe he knew the names of some big hotels in Nairobi that she could try, since she'd never found Pat's file with the addresses and numbers. Then again, maybe Rest Hour would be the best time, although she didn't like to keep dumping her responsibilities on Carol.

Then as she was going to lunch she saw Ham and tried to catch up with him. He didn't see her, but he did something odd. He slipped away from the boys he was with and disappeared around the corner of the Hash House. There was nothing back there except the volleyball and basketball courts and another path that led to the beach. Julie caught hold of Carol's arm and asked her to take her place at the table.

"I don't mean to keep dumping my job on you, but there's something I have to do."

Carol nodded. "I know. Something about Pat. Don't worry, Julie, it's no problem."

Hurrying around to the back of the Hash House, Julie looked for Ham. She caught sight of the top of Ham's head as he went down the incline to the beach. He was carrying something. He looked back over his shoulder, but she ducked behind a bush, and he didn't see her. There was no one else around. From the Hash House she could hear the steady drone of conversation, an occasional laugh, and the clatter of dishes. Everyone was occupied for the time being.

Staying far enough behind Ham so he wouldn't

notice her, she watched as he worked hastily, heaving one of the aluminum canoes off the rack and getting a paddle from the boat house. He waded almost waist-deep into the water and then climbed into the canoe, almost capsizing it in his haste. He knelt in the middle, Indian fashion. Then he pulled off his bright red sweat shirt with the white letters QUESTION AUTHORITY, as if it had occurred to him he might be conspicuous wearing it.

As soon as Ham's canoe disappeared along the shore line, she got herself a canoe and followed him. Vinegar Cove could wait. She wanted to know where he was going. If he was just making a futile search for Pat, she would get him to come back. But if he knew where Pat was . . .

For a while, until he was out of sight of camp, Ham hugged the shore. She did the same, staying far enough behind so as not to alert him. A couple of times he glanced back, but he looked over his right shoulder, and she was keeping to the left of him. In his kneeling position, he couldn't turn all the way around. Once or twice, though, she had to paddle quickly into one of the many little coves to say hidden. Ahead of them, on the other side of the lake, there was a motorboat that looked a little like Rick's, and she noticed he was keeping his eye on that. But then the motorboat speeded up and headed for Vinegar Cove.

She wondered if Ham had stashed away food this time. If Pat were alive on the mountain, or on another mountain, she would be cold and hungry. Another mountain! She hadn't considered that. Pat could have wandered off the trail in the sudden darkness that the storm had caused, and somehow followed the switch-back to Thorne Mountain, or even to that little mountain behind Bear. It was easy to get lost in the woods at night.

She glanced over at Vinegar Cove on the other side of the lake. It looked small and cozy, like a picture on a calendar. If nothing came of following Ham, she would cross over there on her way back and try to phone Nairobi. What an odd life Pat's father led, traveling around the world taking pictures of big game. Why didn't he go somewhere where he could take his child? She was glad she had her parents.

Ham was nearing the beach now, and she held back out of sight. Once he got to the beach, he wouldn't be able to see her until she, too, came around the point past the protecting arm of the cove.

When she got to the beach, Ham was nowhere to be seen. His canoe was pulled up on the sand, the paddle lying carelessly half in and half out of the canoe. Julie beached her own canoe and started up the trail.

She watched the ground, looking for any place where he might have left the narrow path. She didn't see any trampled bushes or footprints in the slightly damp dirt. The smell of pine needles was sharp. A pale sun slanted through the trees, casting shadows, and overhead there were masses of cloud.

She felt uneasy, as if she were being followed, and kept looking back over her shoulder. "You're getting paranoid," she told herself. But she couldn't get rid of the feeling.

The trail got sharply steeper, and she had to stop once or twice to get her breath. The path was a fire trail that didn't get much use. *At least not until a couple of days ago,* she thought.

Suddenly she heard a twig snap. Stopping dead in her tracks, she looked back fearfully. But as far as she could see, there was nothing there.

A few steps further on, Julie came into a low-lying cloud that enveloped her suddenly in blinding, clinging fog. It was terrifying not to be able to see. She felt claustrophobic, and the silence around her seemed ominous, as if something were waiting to spring at her. Panicked, she half turned to start back down the mountain.

To her left, sounding close by, there was a crashing sound. Julie froze.

Chapter 11

She couldn't move. She had never been so scared. It was the not-knowing-what-was-out-there that was so awful. The noise she had heard could be Al, following her to kill her, or Rick, or even Joe or Mark. Everyone seemed like an enemy, Julie thought despondently. She had no right to be here, and with all her heart she wished she could get off the stupid mountain back to the safety of camp—if it was safe, that is.

She tried to tell herself she was being hysterical. She was used to mountains and woods. She had never been afraid of them before. Taking deep breaths to steady herself, Julie realized she was clinging to the rough trunk of a stunted tree so tightly that her hands hurt.

The noise came again. If she could only see! It

couldn't be Ham; it made too much noise, like a large body crashing around in the brush. It had to be an animal. If any person was stalking her, they wouldn't make all that racket. She forced herself to calm down and listen. The noise seemed to have moved off to her right.

The cloud was thinning into wet strands of fog, and she could make out things directly around her now. Feeling a little less anxious, she took a step forward, parted some bushes beside the trail, and found herself staring at a moose.

The animal heard her and wheeled his huge, clumsy body around to face her. He looked enormous. His antlers, still shabby-looking with the last of the season's velvet clinging to them, were at least six feet across.

She stood perfectly still. Usually a moose would not attack except in the mating season, but you never knew for sure, and the mating season was only weeks away. She had heard of people being treed by a moose, but there were no trees here big enough to climb.

Julie held her breath. After what seemed hours, he lowered his head, grabbed a mouthful of ground juniper, and with a heavy half-turn lumbered off, leaving a trail of broken brush behind him.

Slowly she let the breath out of her lungs. The moose had gone in a diagonally downhill direction. She decided she had better keep on going up.

She moved more cautiously now, keeping a sharp lookout all around. She had climbed out of the strands of cloud, but the air was murky and cold. She hadn't come a long way, but it was a hard trail. Her hands were scratched from pulling herself over difficult places. *A little kid like Ham or Pat could scramble up here a lot faster,* Julie thought.

Every sound made her jump. She wished she knew whether or not she was following Ham in the right direction. Instead she was climbing blindly, not knowing where she was going. Her nerves felt raw, and anxiety clicked away in her head like a clock.

If she kept going, she would come to the tarn, Julie knew, but she didn't really think the cave was around there. Of course, there might not even be a real cave. Stories like that spread around till everybody believed them. Ham had said he knew where it was, but he could have been showing off. And would it be big enough for an eleven-year-old girl to hide in anyway?

A broken bush to her left caught Julie's eye. Someone or something had moved off the trail here. Not the moose; there wasn't enough damage. Could it be Ham? She tried to find footprints.

She thought she saw one, but it wasn't clear enough for her to be sure. It could have been an animal print. She stood still, wondering which way to go.

She decided to go as far as she could in the direction that the footprint or animal print led her in. Stepping cautiously off the trail, Julie noted that the air was thinner up here. Bear Mountain was not one of the highest mountains in the area, but the land at the foot of the mountain was already five thousand feet high. Breathing was not as easy up here.

Cloud enveloped her again, wet and clinging. Visibility was close to zero. She moved ahead very carefully, feeling in front of her. It would be only too easy to get lost. And she still had that strange prickling feeling in the back of her neck, as if someone or something threatening were just behind her.

All at once she was above the cloud into clear sunlight, and almost at her feet the ground dropped away for hundreds of feet. She stopped in terror. Another half minute and she would have stepped off that cliff into space. Julie shuddered and took a step backward.

She had a choice: she could go back the way she had come or she could climb a short but almost sheer rise of rock at her right. Her instinct was to turn back. On the other hand, though, the cave might be on that next shelf of level rock above her. Could she risk missing it?

She took a deep breath and immediately wished she hadn't. Some people blacked out when they got up in the mountains. She felt giddy and light-headed. The champagne effect, her father called it.

Looking nervously around her, first Julie studied the

cliff. It was almost covered with lichen, but here and there sturdy-looking bushes grew out of clefts in the rock. Enough for handholds? If one gave way when she was part way up the cliff, she could be thrown into that great void below her. The decision was especially difficult, since she had always stayed away from rock-climbing because of a fear of heights.

Far below her the valley looked like a miniature scene, a long way down. Houses like dollhouses, tiny trees, and the lake like an irregular mirror—it looked unreal.

She shook her head. It must be the altitude that was making her feel so odd. That and the knowledge that she *had* to climb that rock wall. Moving closer to the cliff, she put her hands against it. The dry lichen crumbled at her touch.

She reached up for the lowest bush and tugged at it to see if it would hold. She found a slight indentation for her foot. She stepped up.

Find a handhold, test it, trust it. Dig in your toes. Reach for another handhold, test it, trust it. Don't look down. Don't look down, she chanted to herself, building the words into a rhythm to climb by.

She grew aware of her own raspy breathing, and once when a light breeze stirred her hair, she clung so tightly to the face of the cliff she could feel the gritty pressure against her cheek. The breeze died away, and she reached up again. Time seemed to stop.

Then she reached up and found nothing. It took her a moment to realize that she had come to the top. One more careful step and she flopped over the edge onto solid ground. She lay there on her stomach, chest heaving, eyes closed. Giddiness spun the world around, and her ears roared; her muscles trembled uncontrollably.

A sound reached her. Still unable to sit up, she opened her eyes. Ham was struggling over the rise to her right, carrying a shoulder pack. His face was red and he was breathing hard; he didn't see her. Julie's first reaction was disbelief that he had arrived here without having to climb that rock wall. She had made that awful climb unnecessarily! She tried to call out to him, but for a moment she couldn't make her voice work.

Ham walked away from her toward the base of the next upward thrust of the mountain. He put down his pack, whistled softly, and pushed aside a pile of brush. Then he picked up the pack and disappeared into the mountain.

She got to her feet, still shaking. She could hear the muffled voices. Ham's voice . . . and Pat's! "Pat!" she cried out and started to run, stumbling. At the mouth of the cave she sank to her knees, trembling. "Pat!"

The voices in the cave stopped instantly.

She tried to see inside, but it was dark. "Pat, Ham, it's me, Julie," she cried again.

Ham came out first, cautiously, as if he expected a trap. As he stared at her, Pat pushed past him. She emerged, looking very pale and disheveled, her hair a tangled mess, her face dirty, her clothes torn and dirty. She stared at Julie as if she couldn't believe her eyes.

"Pat, oh, Pat!" Julie held out her arms, and Pat stumbled into them and began to cry.

Still on her knees, Julie rocked the young girl in her arms, her own tears mixing with Pat's. "Pat, Pat, whatever happened?"

"They were going to kidnap her," Ham said. He was unpacking his back pack now. He took out a carton of milk and a couple of sugared doughnuts.

Even as she clung to Julie, Pat grabbed a doughnut and began to eat as if she were starving.

"Drink some milk," Ham told her. He opened the carton and she jammed the rest of the doughnut into her mouth and seized the milk.

"Kidnap?" Julie felt as if her mind weren't working straight. "Kidnap? Who?"

"We heard them," Ham explained. "On the night of the cookout, Rick and Al were supposed to be looking for us—at least that's what Rick told me."

Pat grabbed Ham's arm. "Does he know we heard him?"

"No, 'course not. I wouldn't tell him that. He thinks you fell in the tarn."

Pat began to shiver violently. Julie held her close.

"Please tell me, what did you hear?"

Her voice muffled, Pat said, sniffling, "They had a plot to kidnap me, the last day of camp."

"But what for?" Julie wanted to think they had misunderstood, but Pat wouldn't have gone through three nights in that dark cave unless she believed it.

"For half a million bucks," Ham broke in. "They were going to make her old man pay half a million to get her back."

"You must have misunderstood." It was more than Julie could grasp. The camp director was going to kidnap one of his own campers?

"I told you that's what the grown-ups would say," Pat said sadly to Ham. "I knew they wouldn't believe us."

Earnestly Ham spoke to Julie, making each word clear and distinct, as if she were deaf. "Rick said, 'Pat'll be secure in that cabin. He'll see to that. That's his job. And we shake her old man down for half a million.' And that fat Al said, 'You're sure he'll come through?' And Rick said, 'Of course. She's his only kid. And half a million is nothing to him.' And Al said, 'I wish it was just us. You shouldn't have run in . . .' And right there Rick stopped him. I think he heard us move."

"We were hardly breathing," Pat said. "I was so scared."

"Who was the other one they were talking about?" Julie asked.

"We don't know," Ham replied. "They moved away and we couldn't hear 'em anymore."

"That's why Ham hid me in the cave," Pat said. "He was going to call my dad today. Daddy's back in Nairobi today."

"In Africa," Ham said proudly. "I was gonna call Africa."

Julie held Pat tight, rocking her a little. The pretty little turtleneck was streaked with dirt. It was all so hard to believe, so horrible. When she saw Rick's face in her mind now, that ever-present smile became a vicious leer. And Al—well, she'd never liked Al before, Julie reflected with a shudder. Who was the other one? She was afraid to wonder.

"We've got to get you out of here," she said to Pat.

"Not back to camp." Pat's arms tightened around her neck.

Julie was trying to think. "We'll paddle across the lake to Vinegar Cove. The sheriff's office is there, and telephones and everything. You'll be safe there." She stood up, lifting Pat to her feet.

"How did you get here and find us?" Ham asked. "I was watching. And there wasn't any other canoe."

"I came up the cliff." She pointed toward the place where she had come up.

Ham's eyes widened. "Wow!"

"What if Daddy doesn't have the cash?" Pat said. She still hung on to Julie. "They'll kill me."

"Don't worry. You aren't going to be kidnapped."

"You're safe now," Ham said. "Julie will take care of us."

"Safe as houses," said a voice behind them.

They whirled around, and Pat screamed.

Chapter 12

Al stood there holding a gun in his hand, smiling in a grim way. He looked hot, and there was a long rip in the front of his sport shirt.

"You guys gave us a chase. Got to hand it to you."

Pat was moaning, "No, no, no," fresh tears gathering in her eyes.

Julie pushed Pat behind her. "What do you want?" She was so frightened the words seemed to stick in her throat.

Al laughed. "Half a million apiece. That's not too much to ask for smart kids like that. Worth that price, right?" He glanced back, at a sound. "Plan for one, get two. Not bad."

Julie caught her breath. Joe was coming up the slope

behind Al. Joe had come to save them! Affection and gratitude washed over her in a flood that made her weak in the knees. She *knew* he hadn't meant it when he sounded so tough and uncaring.

Then Joe saw her. "Julie!" All the color faded out of his face.

"Surprise, surprise," Al said in a jeering voice. "It isn't that other fella after all."

Joe had a lariat coiled over his shoulder. He didn't move. It was as if the sight of Julie had paralyzed him.

"Come on," Al said impatiently. "We haven't got all day. Tie up the kids."

Pat was whimpering and saying no, over and over.

Ham was trembling but he took a step toward Al. "You won't get away with it."

Al grinned. "Is that right?" He waved the gun at Ham. "Get back there with your girl friend. Hurry it up, Joe, tie 'em up."

Julie felt as if the whole world had tilted over on its side. Joe was part of the kidnapping scheme. *Joe?*

As if answering her, Joe said, "I couldn't help it, Julie. Rick blackmailed me."

Julie tried to speak, but her throat seemed to close.

Al made a threatening motion toward Joe with his gun. "Do it!"

As Joe moved toward them, making a half-circle to avoid coming close to Julie, Ham cried out.

"Joe! Don't do it, Joe. Don't hurt us."

Joe's face twisted. "Nobody's going to hurt you," he mumbled. "Don't be scared."

Julie turned and caught both children in her arms. "Don't you touch them!" she cried.

He hesitated. "Julie, I can't help it. They won't get hurt, I swear."

"You, Counselor," Al said, his voice rougher than it had been. "Let go of the kids."

"What about Julie?" Joe asked.

"I'll worry about Julie." He waited a moment, and when Julie didn't move he fired a shot into the ground, near her feet. Both children screamed. "Move over here, Counselor. Now. This isn't a game."

"Do it, Julie," Joe said. "He doesn't fool around." He looped the lariat and pulled the children loose from Julie. Then he dropped the loop over their shoulders and pulled it tight as if he were roping a calf.

Al grabbed Julie by the arm and jerked her away from the children. Quickly Joe bound the children together and tied the loose end of the rope around a stunted tree.

"There's nothing like a cowboy," Al remarked, his voice ugly. "All right, Joe, you stay here with the kids while the counselor and I take a little walk." Julie's knees almost buckled under her. *Hang on, hang on,* she told herself. *Try to think logically. Don't go to pieces.*

"Where to?" Joe said.

"Where do you think? She's been real curious about that tarn. We'll give her a chance to see what's in it."

"No!" Joe clenched his fists and stepped toward Al.

Al pointed the gun at him. "Don't lose your head, cowboy."

Julie found her voice. "You won't get away with it. I've already called my father . . . He's district attorney."

Al laughed, a grating sound. "Yeah? Of where? Podunk Heights? Sister, I kept careful track of outgoing calls. You didn't call anybody." He waved his gun at her. "Move."

Pat was ashen, and Ham looked as if he might faint.

Suddenly Joe lunged at Al. But Al was quick. He brought the gun down hard on Joe's head, and Joe sank to the ground, out cold.

While Al's attention was still on Joe, Julie flew at him. She tried to get the gun. It fell from Al's hand and hit the earth with a thud. Furious, he shook Julie off and gave her a hard shove that sent her crashing to the ground.

Al stooped to pick up the gun, and for a moment Julie thought she was hallucinating. Dazed, she watched Mark race up over the hill and tackle Al. For a minute there was complete confusion as Mark and Al struggled against each other. Then Mark had the gun.

"On your feet," he ordered Al, "or I'll fire this thing." There was a streak of blood down the side of his face.

Joe was sitting up, looking completely bewildered.

"Get up, Joe," Mark said.

Both men got slowly to their feet. There was a swollen bruise on Joe's head.

Julie rushed over to untie the children. Joe had tied the knots securely, and her fingers were shaking, but she got the rope untied. Pat sank to the ground in a heap, and Ham leaned over to comfort her.

"You guys." Mark sounded tough as he spoke to Al and Joe. "Stand close together." When they had shuffled close, he said, "Julie, will you hold the gun on them while I tie them up?"

She held the gun with both hands to keep it steady.

Quickly Mark tied Joe and Al together around their arms and waists. He left their legs free so they could walk. Unable to resist, Ham ran to Al and hit him hard in his flabby stomach. Al let out a grunt.

"Ham," Mark said gently, "you and Pat start down the trail."

"Where are we going?" Pat asked.

"We're going to take these guys to the sheriff."

"Rick will kill us," Pat said fearfully.

"No, he won't. Take it easy, Pat."

"It's all right, it really is," Julie told Pat, even though she could hardly believe it *was* all right. A minute ago she had been on her way to her death, and the children to who knew what horror. Then Mark had come and everything was under control. It struck her in a blinding flash that she loved him.

Ham helped Pat on the way down. Mark herded Joe and Al in front of him, keeping the rope looped around his arm and held tightly in his hand. Julie kept the gun trained on Al. She hoped he couldn't guess that she would never shoot anybody.

As they descended, she saw the place on the mountain where she had gone off on a tangent. This way was much faster and easier. She couldn't believe she had climbed that cliff for nothing.

As they walked, she tried to keep her mind on Al and Joe. But it was an effort, because all the while, in her head, *I love Mark!* kept ringing and ringing like Christmas bells.

Chapter 13

As they came to the beach at last, Ham let out a yell of delight. "He brought Rick's boat! We can use the motorboat."

Mark kept the rope in his hand as he and Ham pushed the motorboat back into the water all the way. Julie stood close to them, feeling uneasy, keeping her eyes on Al. If Al was going to make a break for it, she figured this would probably be the time, since Mark's attention was distracted. Then she saw that Joe had braced his feet and was leaning his weight backward, keeping Al slightly off balance, and a wave of compassion swept over her. Poor Joe, she thought, he's trying to make up for what he's done. How did he get into such a mess? He was avoiding looking at her.

Mark herded Al and Joe into the boat and tied the rope around the seat amidship. Julie and the children sat in the bow, facing Al and Joe. Mark pushed off and climbed into the boat, started the motor, and steered in the direction of Vinegar Cove.

No one spoke on the crossing. Pat sat huddled in Julie's lap, and Ham held her hand tightly in his two small hands. The sun was just beginning its serene glide toward the west. The water was calm, glittering here and there as the sunlight struck it. A day made for swimming and boating and hiking, Julie thought. What was happening didn't seem real. But the cold metal of the heavy gun in her hand was real enough. The bitter sullenness on Al's face was real.

As Mark brought the boat alongside the town dock, a boy who was fishing from the end of the dock stared at them. He jumped up and guided the bow alongside as Mark cut the motor.

"What's up?" the boy said.

"Which way is the sheriff's office?" Mark asked him.

The boy jerked a hand. "First place on your left." He spoke to Ham. "Is this a movie or is it for real?"

"It's for real," Ham told him, importantly. Motioning toward Al, he added, "The fat one's with the mob."

Mark looked at Julie, a flash of smile lighting up his face.

"We captured him." Pat spoke up, scrambling out of

144

the boat. She was beginning to sound like herself, Julie thought with relief.

"Is there a reward?" the boy asked, impressed. He grabbed the painter and tied it to a mooring post.

"Probably," Ham said. "We'll split it."

Mark jerked the rope as Al and Joe climbed out of the boat. The boy trailed after them as they walked up the street, a strange procession that soon brought people out of the stores to look. Julie felt like an actress in a grade B Western.

As they neared the station, the boy ran ahead to alert the sheriff.

By the time they reached the small building with the tin roof and the false front, the sheriff was coming out the door. He was a big man in scuffed boots and a blue denim shirt and jeans. His badge glittered in the sun.

He squinted at the odd group. "What we got here?"

Julie handed him the gun. "This man"—she pointed to Al, ignoring Joe—"was trying to kidnap these children. He was going to kill me."

"Well, well," the sheriff said. "Come inside and have a seat."

The tiny office seemed crowded with all of them in it. The deputy, a short, dark-complexioned Indian whom the sheriff introduced as Hank Running Boy, sat on a chair positioned backward on the threshold between the outer office and Sheriff Woodley's office. He took notes as the children, then Julie, and finally Mark told what they knew of the things that had been going on. Joe stood with his back to them, shoulders hunched, staring out the window. Al leaned against the wall, only half paying attention to what was said, or so it seemed. As if he were at a boring play, Julie thought.

Al shrugged when the sheriff asked if he had anything to say. But Joe said, "I didn't want to do it. Rick threatened me. He . . . he had something on me." He shot a miserable glance at Julie. "He swore they wouldn't get hurt."

"You're the football fella," the sheriff said.

"Was," Joe said bitterly. "That's shot."

"You want to tell us what he had on you?"

Joe didn't answer for a moment. "Guess it doesn't matter now." He looked away from the children. "I threw the South Dakota game," he said and then his voice broke.

There was silence in the room. Then Pat leaned forward and touched his arm. "We like you anyway, Joe."

He started to speak. His eyes filled with tears, and he turned away. Al gave a scornful snort.

The sheriff offered the men a phone call, but they both refused it. "Well," he said to his deputy, "I guess we got an empty cell, haven't we, Hank?"

"Yes, sir."

"Why don't you stash these boys away, and then I got a notion these kids could use one of Cecil's hamburgers. You might take these good folks over there while I do a little calling around."

Hank nodded and came back a moment later with two pairs of handcuffs.

Ham watched, fascinated. "Can I come while you lock 'em up?"

"Don't see why not."

"You come too, Pat," Ham suggested, but Pat shook her head.

"Did Search and Rescue notify you about Pat's disappearance?" Mark asked the sheriff.

"Never heard a word. Which means neither did they. It'd be routine for them to notify me."

They all looked at Joe. Hank was adjusting his handcuffs.

"Rick thought we'd find her," Joe said. "He didn't believe she'd drowned. After all, the body would've surfaced by this time."

Pat shivered and grabbed Julie's hand.

"He figured she overheard him and Al talking about the snatch, and that she hid out. He didn't want her spilling the beans to Search and Rescue."

Al shot him a venomous look. "Why don't you shut that big mouth?" he growled.

"What happened to the file on Pat?" Julie said.

"Rick locked it up in his desk. He was afraid you'd start calling the kid's relatives. That's why I searched the trunks, in case there was an address book."

"Thought of everything, didn't he?" the sheriff asked dryly.

"There was a lot at stake," Joe said.

"All right, Hank, take these gentlemen away." The sheriff turned to Pat after Hank had herded the prisoners out of the office. "I guess your daddy's going to be proud of you, young lady. You outsmarted some real nasty crooks."

Pat nodded her head, a half smile on her lips. "I guess Ham and I saved Daddy a lot of money," she said shyly. Then she looked anxious again. "You'll catch Rick, won't you?"

"You betcha." He turned to Julie. "If the little girl would like to clean up, there's a washroom out there to your right."

When Pat and Julie came back, Hank and Mark were waiting. As they walked to the hamburger place, Julie said to Mark, "That flashlight of yours, I was wondering about it. Remember, when it went off and then came on again . . ."

He grinned. "You thought I was faking it, right?" Julie nodded blushingly. "It was just what I told you; Ham wore down the battery."

"I had to use it a lot," Ham broke in. "It got so dark all of a sudden, when I was taking Pat to the cave."

Mark took Julie's hand, and a ripple of pleasure went through her. It seemed like the most natural and right thing that she could imagine. All the tension and worry and fear that had weighed her down for the last few days vanished.

Ham glanced back at them, then whispered something to Pat. She glanced back and both of them giggled. Mark smiled at Julie.

"Looks like they know something we don't know," he said.

"*I* know it," Julie said and blushed again.

He tightened his grip on her hand.

In the café Pat ate steadily and silently—french fries, a thick hamburger with onion and pickle, onion rings, milk. Ham ate as he always did, with enthusiasm. Hank drank his coffee in silence except for a few exchanges with Cecil, the tall, lanky proprietor. Julie and Mark were left in a little island where only each other existed.

"You thought I was in on it, didn't you?" Mark said softly. He was still holding her hand, and they both laughed at the difficulties of managing a hamburger with one hand.

"I don't think I really did. Just once in a while I wondered, because you always seemed to be there."

"So did you." He grinned at her. "But I didn't suspect you. Know what?"

"What?"

"Well, I was keeping an eye on you . . ."

She interrupted him. "You did suspect me!"

". . . keeping an eye on you so you wouldn't get hurt!"

"Oh. Mark . . ."

Hank leaned toward them and said with a straight

face, "I got a notion these kids want at least one more hamburger. If you folks'd like to see the local sights, there's a real pretty little cove just up the road. I'll mind the young 'uns."

Mark grinned. "Thanks, pal."

They walked up the dirt road, past the laundromat and the Silver Dollar bar, past the sporting goods store and the barbershop, to the end of the town. A small rickety dock leaned into the water; a couple of paint-faded rowboats were tied to it, and a flat-bottomed dory was overturned on the dock.

For a few minutes they just stood close together, holding hands, staring out at the lake. Then Mark said, "You know that expression about seeing red . . ."

"Yes."

"I always thought it was just something people said. But when I saw that creep knock you down, I saw red. I mean literally. Like a red cloud across my eyes. Then—I'll tell you about another common expression—about seeing your past life flash by? Well, I saw my future flash by. Saw it all."

She felt breathless. "How did it look?"

He dropped her hand and put his arm around her. "It looked great. You and me, we were the principal characters. In every scene." He laughed a happy laugh and hugged her close to him.

"What were we doing?" she asked and blushed.

"You're blushing."

"I haven't blushed since I was ten years old . . . until today."

"Tell me why."

"While you were having all those visions up on the mountain, red clouds and the future and all that, I looked at you and I thought . . ." She hesitated.

"Thought what?"

"I thought, I love him!"

He put both arms around her and kissed her. "Julie."

She leaned back a little and looked at him. Then she took his face between her hands and kissed him.

"Do you really have a sailboat with striped sails?" she said.

"My brother does."

"Do you really live in a place called Marblehead?"

"Do you really live in a place called White-*fish?*"

"Come and see," she said.

"Come and see yourself. How's the air service out of Montana?"

"Terrible."

"Then we'll just have to hitchhike."

Someone behind them coughed.

"Here we go again," Julie said.

Ham and Pat were giggling and Hank was trying to look as if he didn't notice a thing.

"They caught Rick," Ham announced, trying to keep a straight face.

Julie looked at Hank. "Really? So soon?"

"The telephone is a great instrument," Hank commented. "He was boarding a plane in Kalispell."

Pat danced around them. "I'm safe. I'm safe, we're all safe." She hugged Julie, and then Hank, and then Ham, who turned bright red and sputtered. "And Julie and Mark are going to get married! Hurray!" she said.

"Hold on," Julie said. "I haven't even started college yet."

"He'll wait," Pat said wisely. "Won't you, Mark?"

"You talked me into it." Mark put his arm around Julie again.

"Oh, gross!" Ham said and ran off down the road.

"He's just a child," Pat said. "He'll change."

For the first time Hank Running Boy laughed. "You got something there, little girl. Uh, I think Sheriff Woodley wants to see you folks for a few minutes. There's stuff to be signed, complaints and all."

"Back to the real world," Mark said as he and Julie walked down the road.

Pat danced along beside them. "Wait till I tell the kids!"

Is sixteen too young to feel the . . .

Romance, excitement, adventure—this is the combination
that makes *Dawn of Love* books so special, that sets them
apart from other romances.

Each book in this new series is a page-turning story
set against the most tumultuous times in America's past—
when the country was as fresh and independent as its daring,
young sixteen-year-old heroines.

Dawn of Love is romance at its best, written to
capture your interest and imagination, and guaranteed to
sweep you into high adventure with love stories you will
never forget.

Here is a glimpse of the first *Dawn of Love* books.

#1 RECKLESS HEART
Dee Austin

The time is 1812, and wild and beautiful Azalee la Fontaine,
the sixteen-year-old daughter of a wealthy New Orleans
shipowner, is used to getting her own way. There's a war with
England going on, and Azalee is warned to curb her reckless
ways, but her daring and scandalous behavior makes her a
prisoner in more ways than one. While the pirate captain Jean
Lafitte can save her from one danger, only Johnny Trent—
Azalee's fiery young man in blue—can tame her heart.

**Look for DAWN OF LOVE historical romances
at your local bookstore!**

Archway Paperbacks, Published by Pocket Books

First Love from Silhouette

THE MOST POPULAR TEEN ROMANCES PUBLISHED TODAY

The books that you have enjoyed all these years with characters so real they seem like friends, and stories so engrossing that you have begged for more!

4 TITLES A MONTH

Stories that mirror your hopes, your dreams, your relationships — the books that you have claimed as your own ever since we first published them.

AT YOUR FAVORITE BOOKSTORE

First Love from Silhouette

FL-A-1